Fiona Tarr

Delilah and the Dark God

Book 2

The Eternal Realm

Books by Fiona Tarr

The Covenant of Grace Series

Book 1 – Destiny of Kings

Book 2 – Seed of Hope

Book 3 – Legacy of Power

Book 4 – Heir of Vengeance

Book 5 – The Ehud Dagger – Prequel Novella

The Eternal Realm Series

Book 1—The Jericho Prophecy

Book 2—Delilah and the Dark God

The Priestess Chronicles Series

Book 1—Call of the Druids

# Chapter 1

'Delilah! Where have you been?' The plump woman with kind eyes pleaded to her daughter as she came rushing through the front door, breathing heavily.

'The temple mother.'

'You know I do not like it when you go to that place. It is foreboding, with the darkness of evil gods.' The woman wrung her hands, concern evident in the creases of her brow.

'Better than chasing the boys though, right mother?' The young woman had the look of mischief on her face and her mother scowled at her brazen behaviour.

'You will be the death of me child. Can you not settle down and find yourself a husband? Your father cannot possibly offer you to anyone if you keep roaming the streets looking like a peasant.'

The woman studied her daughter's bare feet, covered with ground-in dirt and filthy toe nails. Her threadbare tunic was virtually see-through and fell far too low as it crossed her cleavage.

'We *are* peasants mother. Father lost his position in the palace months ago. Remember! That is what happens when you do not simply agree with everything the King wants.' The girl took a deep breath, puffed out her chest and placed her hands firmly on her hips.

'Hush Delilah.' The woman looked over her shoulder apprehensively. 'You speak treason. Are you trying to get us both killed?'

'That is right mother. They will not kill father, just his Hebrew whore and half-breed daughter.'

'By all that is Holy child, keep your voice down.' The woman's eyes grew wide with fear and she looked around the room as though a spy or soldier could fall upon them at any moment.

'Next you will be saying for Yahweh's sake. Now that *could* get us both killed.' Delilah grabbed a shrivelled and dry bunch of grapes from the wooden bowl on the worn table and studied them for pests and mould before throwing them one by one greedily into her mouth as she made to leave.

'Where are you going?' Her mother moved as if to bar the doorway.

'Some place where I do not have to listen to your ranting of course.' The girl squeezed past and looked over her shoulder smiling casually to soften her words. She took one look back over her shoulder as she cleared the doorway of the rough, sun baked adobe shelter she now called home.

****

'I have this. You cannot possibly win. You should just give up before I break your arm or worse.' The veins were bulging on the man's neck, but his breathing was smooth and he had barely broken a sweat as he challenged his adversary.

'You better listen to Aviv my friend. He is mighty strong.' The handsome broad-shouldered Israelite alongside the wrestler smiled as he goaded Aviv's opponent.

'I am not your friend. You… Israelites…. are all the same. Over… confident….' The soldier grunted out each word as sweat beaded on his brow. The combatant's fists were clasped as they arm-wrestled on a weathered wooden table.

Onlookers from the market had stopped to watch the spectacle, and many had placed random bets with the tavern owner and were now beginning to shout words of encouragement to their chosen victor.

Aviv's knuckles were white with the strain but he was winning, slowly, until something exotic caught his eye. It was only a heartbeat before he saw his mug of ale fly into the air as his fist rammed through it and onto the table with a thud.

The crowd exploded with a mix of cheers and angry growls. A fight broke out beyond the dining area and everyone moved to place another wager.

'Ah, there. I told you that you were over confident.' The Philistine soldier jumped up from the bench and held his hand out to collect his winnings.

The big man ignored him. 'What happened Aviv? You had him!'

'I did Samson, until I saw her.' Aviv nodded outside the tavern courtyard to his distraction. 'Pay him Samson, I have better things to do.' Aviv moved out to pursue his prey.

'What? No, this was your wager.' Samson pouted after his friend as disgruntled punters began to protest that the Israelite had thrown the fight and they wanted their money back.

Samson merely scowled in their direction and they quickly dispersed, thinking better of the challenge.

'Pay up big man.' The soldier demanded, undeterred.

'Double or nothing? I bet I can take you!' Samson grinned, but his eyes followed his friend's distraction, her hips swayed seductively making it difficult to focus on the task at hand.

'I do not think so Samson. Your reputation precedes you. A Judge of the Israelites should not be betting in any case.'

'Ah, gone are the days when I could enjoy myself and remain anonymous.' Samson opened his small drawstring pouch and pulled out the payment. 'I should have known better than to bet on Aviv.'

The Soldier laughed as he collected his winnings. 'Lucky for me he is easily distracted by a pretty woman.'

'Yes, good point. I had better catch him before she slaps him, or worse.' Samson set off after Aviv at a quick pace. He caught up to him in the main market square as his friend valiantly bartered with a fruit vendor on the woman's behalf.

'Fruit? That is unlike you Aviv.' Samson pushed through the growing crowd and drew up alongside his friend.

'Nonsense. I love fruit.' Aviv looked the young woman in the eye and smiled charismatically as he lied.

'Excuse my friend's bad manners. I do not believe we have met?' Samson bowed and waited for an introduction.

The girl batted her eyelashes and opened her mouth to speak, just as Samson was pushed forward, almost landing in the fruit stand. It rocked precariously for a moment before he steadied it with a strong hand.

'What on earth?' The big man turned around to complain.

'Get out of the way, you, you big oaf.'

Aviv and Samson exchanged confused glances and Samson stepped back out of the way of the young woman who had in all reality barged into him.

'I do apologise. I failed to see you there.' Samson bowed to emphasise his apology.

'Hmm!' The woman shrugged and put her hands on her hips defiantly. Samson could not help but notice her tunic was almost sheer. Her nipples were practically visible through the fabric and it was extremely difficult to keep his eyes on her face.

'No harm done I guess.' She moved on quickly and Aviv returned his attention to the woman with the pretty eyelashes.

Samson moved away from his friend, his eyes following the young woman as she wove her way through the thickening mid-day market crowd.

Sorek was a remote, but bustling trading town in the valley of Sorek and Samson seldom visited the area. If not for the local disputes he adjudicated over, he would never have found this beautiful place with its stone streets and white painted buildings.

The aroma of cooking meat and fresh fruit flooded Samson's senses and the market was full of merchants, soldiers and local orchard workers making it difficult to stay focussed.

He lost sight of the woman, but her dark eyes and pert nipples remained ingrained in his memory. He shook his head to force himself back to the present as Aviv's voice invaded his daydreams.

'Samson, can you pay the merchant for the fruit?' Aviv nodded toward the fruit stand owner and grinned, winking in a way that left no misunderstanding who his friend was trying to impress.

Samson reached for his bag of coin and felt nothing. He frantically patted himself down, seeking the coin purse. Within seconds his eyes had darted to the ground as he began to retrace his steps back to the tavern.

'Where are you going?' Aviv called after him.

'My coin! I have lost my coin.' The fruit merchant reached out and snatched the basket of fruit as the woman with the pretty eyes lifted her chin, huffed and moved on as though she had never met Aviv.

Aviv sighed and pouted before chasing after his friend, dodging around stands and merchants as he caught up.

'Where did you last have it?'

'When I paid *your* wager.' Samson did not attempt to keep the contempt from his voice.

'You sure you tied it back when you finished?' Aviv struggled to keep up with Samson as the big man took long, quick steps, his frustration evident in every footfall.

'Of course I….. No! She cannot have!' Samson lifted his head and peered into the crowd once more. His eyes scanned the vast array of brightly coloured foreigners that flocked to trade in this border town. Finally, ceasing his search as realisation sunk in... 'She took it. That little minx took my coin purse.'

Chapter 2

Delilah ducked into the darkened alley away from prying eyes and untied the cord of the thick canvas purse. She poured the contents out into her hand and studied the coins a moment, almost shocked at her good fortune. She let out a low whistle as she counted the five gold, ten silver and a handful of copper pieces in the palm of her hand.

She scanned her surroundings protectively and hastily replaced the coins in the bag, before tying it around her inner thigh. She smirked as she smoothed her tunic into place and left the alley.

The smell of fresh flowers and urine drifted to Delilah as she moved down the weaving pathways that littered the town.

When her father had first moved them to Sorek, Delilah had been mortified. Gone were her splendid clothes and the fine banquets of Philistine royal society. Instead she was faced with dirty streets and sheep markets.

There would be no more high ranking officers or men of means trying to win her hand in marriage. She had been depressed and sullen for some time but now, she found herself relishing the adventure and adrenalin that came with the life of a pauper.

The street ahead continued to wind around almost in a circle it seemed and Delilah wondered if anyone had intentionally designed this town or it had just expanded randomly with time. She decided the latter was most likely as she wove her way down yet another alley to eventually find the temple before her.

As the young woman entered, the Acolyte near the altar winked in her direction. Delilah licked her lips in response and the Acolyte with the handsome face and neatly manicured side-burns pouted his lips seductively.

Delilah laughed quietly and returned her attention to the business at hand. The Sorek temple was not as large as the one in Gaza, where Delilah had once resided, but it was relatively unregulated and Delilah revelled in the freedom.

'What offering do you bring the lord Dagon today Delilah?' An old balding man with hunched shoulders approached the young woman who bowed reverently in response. He gazed longingly at the gap in her tunic as she dropped down, her head raised so as not to interrupt his view.

'A coin purse Lord, with a generous speckling of gold for a change.' Delilah lifted her dress unashamedly, smiling at the young Acolyte who was cleaning candle sticks nearby craning his neck for a mere glimpse. The old priest pursed his lips and resisted the urge to reach out and touch her bronze thigh.

'Did you keep any for yourself child?' He asked not taking his eyes from her leg.

'Of course not Lord.' Delilah knew she needed to be convincing and she had practised the look of innocence. If the old man suspected anything he would think nothing of searching every orifice of her person just to ensure she kept her word.

The Priest opened the bag as he walked over to the thick stone altar and scattered the contents on the rough surface. The coins rolled until they struck the blood channels and well-worn knife marks. Delilah resisted the urge to cringe as she saw a speck of blood had been forgotten by the cleaners.

'Hmm. Three gold pieces, fine indeed. You are right; we do not see many of these. Eight silver too. You did well Delilah. The lord Dagon will reward you in this life or the next.'

The girl dropped to her knees before the altar to accept the Priest's blessing and tried unsuccessfully not to shudder at the touch of his shockingly cold hands.

****

The woman greeted her husband with a hug and made her way to the hearth to stir the meal she had been preparing.

'Where is Delilah?' He asked as he poured water into a chipped clay bowl and washed his hands before splashing his face.

'Out again. We had another argument.'

He shook his hands as he looked for a cloth, finding it waiting in his wife's outstretched hand.

'We must find her a husband Amariah, before she grows too reckless and there is only one profession left to her.' The man sighed as he wiped the water from his face and tossed the cloth onto the closest surface.

'Never Fajer. How could you ever consider handing her over to the temple like that?' Amariah poured a watery broth into a wooden bowl and placed it before her husband on the table, avoiding the long crack that ran down the centre.

'Do not be blind woman, she is already serving them. It is only a matter of time before they put her to work for some rich noble.' Fajer sat carefully on the rickety bench. He ensured he was stable before pouring the thin liquid over the spoon mournfully and placing some in his mouth.

Amariah stifled a cry at her husband's callous words. It was his fault they were in this forsaken place. 'Why did you have to disagree with the King, Fajer? Why?' She tried not to cry, but the tears rose unbidden.

The man stopped himself from retaliating as his wife broke down again. 'Come now Amariah. We will find her a husband. She is a beautiful young woman.' Fajer rose from the seat and wrapped his arm around his wife.

'Yes,' the woman sniffled, 'far too beautiful Fajer.' Amariah leant into her husband's arms and they consoled each other for a moment.

'Surely the King will allow you to return. A time in exile, then an apology?'

'I do not think so Amariah. Besides, our time is near, returning to the service of the King now would only prove dangerous. Your people are growing restless with the yoke of the Philistines and we are in no man's land here. We need to tread carefully. Philistines and Israelites were not supposed to wed for just this reason. Our people will never know lasting peace.'

'There are prophecies that would argue with you, husband. Our people hope for a messiah, from the line of Kings.'

'Preposterous, Israel has no King. Blind faith from Priests who know nothing of the real world; too busy reading ancient scrolls and kissing their fists to dribble on their own foreheads in prayer.' Fajer returned to his broth and forced a spoonful into his mouth.

'Let us not turn this into a fight of the faiths. You know Delilah is worshiping at the temple and Dagon is dangerous. The Israelites might be blind with their faith at times, but they do not sacrifice virgins to their god.' Amariah's cheeks grew flushed at the thought of her daughter being chosen for such a rite.

'Nothing but an old wives' tale woman. When was the last human sacrifice held in the temple?' Fajer swallowed another spoonful and sighed his discontent.

'I hate to consider it. I am sure we do not know of them. They would be held in secret like everything that goes on in that temple. Why else would Delilah be so absorbed in being there every day? You mark my words Fajer, you ignore this, and we may very well lose our daughter to Dagon, one way or another.'

'I hear you Amariah. I will find her a husband. I promise.' The man sighed in resignation. There was no point arguing with his wife when she got these silly notions into her head.

Fajer adjusted his position on the precarious seat and lifted his bowl to his lips, ignoring the wooden spoon.

Chapter 3

'Why would she take my coin Aviv?'

'Did you see her tunic Samson? Hunger might have something to do with it?' Aviv offered good-naturedly. 'You hold no jurisdiction here my friend. This is a Philistine matter. If she was an Israelite, maybe you could do something'

Samson mulled over Aviv's words without comment. 'Tell me you brought coin with you?'

'Yes, of course I did.' Aviv raised his hands, palm upwards. 'How stupid do you think I am?'

'Then why was I paying for everything?' Samson stopped walking and looked at his friend in confusion.

'Because you are a Judge and I am shepherd.'

'So!'

'You get paid more than me and since I am your closest friend—no make that your only friend—you know you do not exactly attract many friends—I thought you could foot the bill today.'

'Well it seems your plan was not the wisest.'

'The plan was fine; you just needed to keep your eyes on your coin purse instead of that girl's chest.' Aviv elbowed Samson in the ribs and grunted as he hit what felt like solid rock. He reached up and gently squeezed his friend's bicep admiringly as they continued making their way toward their lodging.

Aviv was considered a strong man, but Samson was another level of strength no one really understood. He was tall with rippling muscles but none of that truly explained his phenomenal power.

'Seriously! You cannot exactly talk. If you had not had a roving eye we would have won that arm-wrestle.' Samson pulled his arm from his friend's hand and frowned uncomfortably at the attention.

'True. I will give you that, but she was beautiful.'

'Who?'

Aviv thought for a moment as one eyebrow rose and his eyes glazed over. 'Both really, in different ways. Mine was refined, splendidly dressed and that eye-liner she wore. Prrrr!'

'Well mine was naturally beautiful. Besides you could never afford to keep yours.' Samson nudged his friend in the ribs and Aviv nearly lost his footing. Samson reached out and clasped his arm before he landed in the dirt. 'Sorry about that.'

The two men rounded the corner before the inn they had taken lodgings in and Samson stopped so fast, Aviv nearly slammed into him.

'What is it?' Aviv asked as he leant around his friend's bulking frame to get a view.

'Soldiers!'

'They do not look happy.'

Two soldiers stood guard while four more paced back and forth obviously waiting for something or someone.

'No, they must have found out I am in town. That damned soldier you wrestled with, he knew my name but he was so calm and courteous that he did not seem interested in causing trouble.'

'I should not have used your name. He was smart enough to not challenge you alone. It looks like he got reinforcements. There is no way any Philistine soldier is going to let you walk out of Sorek after what you did.'

'That was twenty years ago and they deserved it.'

Aviv pursed his lips and nodded his head from side to side as he considered Samson's words. 'Well I guess you can say some of them deserved it but you did go a little berserk you know.'

'I only had a donkey's jaw-bone. Seriously! They had swords.'

'Yes, that they did, but you probably did not need to kill every man there, especially those who had cut and run.'

'They deserved it even more.'

'Why?' Aviv spread his hands and shook his head in confusion.

'*Because* they ran.'

'I rest my case. Only one friend for a reason and I am still not sure why I hang around.'

'For the women.'

Aviv raised his eyebrows in momentary thought and nodded. 'Yes, there is that.'

'We need to find that girl.' Samson changed the subject and turned to leave the inn but he was too late.

'There he is! Get him!' Soldiers ran from the cobbled stone square in front of their accommodation.

'Damn' Aviv muttered. 'Try not to kill anyone Samson.'

'I will do my best.'

Aviv stepped back to give the warrior room. He had seen this scenario unfold too many times to remember them all.

The first man met Samson's fist with his jaw. The sound of the crack sent shivers down Aviv's spine and the man fell to the ground unconscious. The second soldier raised his sword against the unarmed Israelite but he wore leather bracers on his forearms and repelled the weapon before lifting the man from his feet with an upper-cut.

Four more assailants jumped on the warrior together, hoping to weigh him down and subdue him.

'It has been tried before my friends.' Aviv smiled at the soldier on top from the sidelines, fully aware of the outcome of this well used strategy.

The soldier had no time to answer before all four men flew into the air, ejected from Samson's back with ease. They fell about the street like knuckle bones and did not rise.

'Time to leave my friend.' Samson started to run without further explanation. We need to find the girl.'

'How?' Aviv called after him, as they sprinted down an alley and around a corner, hoping to lose any further pursuers.

'I have no idea. What about you?' Samson called back, smiling with the excitement despite the danger.

They took two more quick side alleys, climbed over a low wall and rushed by dozens of market stalls before taking another side alley. Confident they had lost their enemy, the men stopped to catch their breath.

'No money and no way of getting any. A shepherd and an Israelite Judge are not exactly in high demand in Sorek you know. You already did what you came for.' Aviv considered their options.

'Yes, but I might be able to get a very small advance from Nesta and if I can, maybe you can wrestle someone for a win?' The big man did not even seem to have broken a sweat and his breathing was already returning to normal.

'All brawn and no brain. How did you become a Judge anyway? Really!'

'What?' Samson shrugged his confusion.

'I think a bribe to find the girl might be a better use of the funds if you can raise them.' Aviv looked out from the alley. Samson nodded toward the soldiers who were milling around the market square, asking questions.

There was a window to a raised walkway above their heads, but well out of reach. Samson smiled and Aviv shook his head.

'No, not again. Last time you hoisted me that high I broke my arm.'

'True but you were distracted. This time, you need to focus. Spot your landing Aviv.'

Samson held out his hands and Aviv shook his head, giving up on the argument. He placed his foot into the big man's hand and held his shoulders as Samson counted.

'One…..two….three.' With that he released his friend into the air.

Aviv tried not to squeal but the sound escaped his lips involuntarily. The balcony was high and Aviv was ultimately scared of heights but he was not about to admit it to Samson.

He reached for the stone railing and clamoured up to safety. As he turned around, he saw Samson take a run and jump at the walkway. He managed to reach a pillar of the balustrading and pulled himself easily to the landing.

'We should take the long way around to the temple and find Nesta. Soldiers will be looking for me.'

'Alright, when it comes to battles you might be brighter, but when it comes to finances I think I have you.'

Samson frowned at his friend. 'But you just finished saying I make more coin than you.'

'Yes, you do but it is not how much you make my friend it is what you do with it that counts. I have two houses you know.'

'What! Only because you make me pay for everything.'

Aviv suddenly realised he might have shared too much. 'Yes, of course, but you are welcome in either anytime Samson. You know this. One in Gaza and one in Jerusalem. Anytime!'

Samson shrugged and moved on. 'Gaza you say?'

'Gaza.'

'The weather is fine in Gaza this time of year.'

'It is.' Aviv sighed in relief and patted the big man on the back as the temple came into view.

****

The Priest replaced his robe and collected the coin from the altar leaving Delilah still on her knees. He enjoyed such blessings. They were two-fold. The girl was now blessed by Dagon and he was refreshed for the evening rituals and arduous work of training stupid young Acolytes.

Delilah rinsed her mouth and spat the contents into the blood drains on the altar before collecting her copper coin from the stone surface. 'So generous you old pig.' She spoke aloud without realising anyone was near.

'You are too beautiful to be serving the Priest when you can be serving Dagon himself Delilah.'

'Wait, let me guess, you are Dagon in disguise as an Acolyte and I can service you, instead of that old balding priest.' Delilah did not try to hold her disdain as she wiped her mouth on the back of her hand and spat on the ground.

She took a breath to compose herself. It was not the Acolyte's fault the priest wanted to 'bless' her. Besides, he was handsome and if she were to give up her virginity soon to avoid the sacrificial altar then he was as good as a peasant girl could expect.

'No, that is not what I meant Delilah. You come here with coin and you hand it to the Priest but you do not pray to Dagon. You do not know him.' The Acolyte's face was so innocent, even with his striking jawline and carefully manicured facial hair.

'What is your name?' Delilah changed the subject, preferring not to talk of matters of faith. Dagon's temple was a means of survival and nothing more. Yahweh had deserted her family, she was not about to launch into swearing fealty to another god or religion.

'Kaamill, my name is Kaamill and I am at your service Delilah. You are as beautiful as the goddess herself.' The Acolyte looked wistfully into the young woman's eyes.

'Which goddess?'

'Dagon's wife, Asherah.'

'Asherah… she sounds beautiful.'

'Oh, she is.'

'How do you know? Have you ever seen her?'

'No, of course not, but there are statues and engravings in the temple. Here, I will show you.'

Kaamill moved away toward the far wall and Delilah followed. She had never wandered around the temple, always focussed on delivering her coin.

No one stole in Sorek without either the approval of the temple or the Guild of Thieves. It always amazed Delilah that thieves could be as organised as politicians and kings, with their own society and leadership to keep the 'rules'. Delilah believed she had chosen the lesser of two evils, but each visit to the temple made her questions that choice.

'See, here she is. This is Asherah.' Kaamill pointed to a carving in the stone depicting a tree shaped like a woman, with heavy bosom and rounded hips, a baby birthing at her feet.

'What makes you believe she is Dagon's wife?' Delilah traced her hand over the depiction of the goddess and smiled as her fingers tingled.

'Here, see this.' Kaamill ran his hand from the image of Asherah to a tree at the water's edge. In the water, the image of Dagon, half-man, half-fish held out his hand to the tree.

'I think that is just Dagon being wishful.' Delilah laughed aloud as the Acolyte gasped.

'That is blasphemous.'

'Only if you can prove that Asherah is Dagon's wife, then it would be, but you cannot, not really.'

'I always thought it to be true.' Kaamill smiled shyly and dropped his eyes.

'A romantic then. Why do you aspire to be a priest of the temple?' Delilah was suddenly genuinely curious.

'Men like me are no different from women like you Delilah. I am not built to be a farmer or a warrior. If I do not become a priest, I will be offered as a concubine and women in Sorek cannot afford such services. I have no wish to be in the service of men.'

Delilah shuddered as she understood the young man's plight. 'At least the beautiful can be well paid for their service, unlike the poor wretches who live in the dirtier part of town where I now reside.'

'You are a princess amongst peasants Delilah. You will find a way. Dagon will take care of you, just ask him.'

'Maybe I will,' The young woman placed her hand on Kaamill's and grinned mischievously, 'but then again, I might choose to worship Asherah.' The Acolyte gasped once more and then smiled as he understood the jest.

'I must go Kaamill, but thank you for showing me this wall. I think I will spend more time here on my next visit.'

The Acolyte bowed reverently. 'My pleasure. Truly Delilah, I am at your service. Anything you should need, simply ask of me and if I can deliver it I will.'

'Thank you.' Delilah's cheeks grew uncharacteristically red and she lowered her gaze, moving away with haste.

She rushed from the temple, stepping out into the large paved square that was the only one of its kind in Sorek. The temple of Israel stood stoically on the opposite side, as though fighting for acceptance

amongst what was predominately a Philistine strong-
hold, but being so close to the border and full of
travelling merchants, the temple had begun to thrive.

Kaamill watched the girl leave and smirked.
'You are a beauty Delilah and you have no idea what I
have in store for you.' The Acolyte's body began to
shimmer as dark charcoal-coloured wings extended
from his back and his form doubled in size. The one
tattoo on his forearm grew as more ornate designs
appeared all over his now bare back.

'Lord, I had no idea you were attending today.'
The Priest heard more than felt Dagon's wings flex in
agitation.

'It is obvious you did not know, or you would
not have had my beautiful Delilah on her knees before
you.' Dagon moved forward, a sharp finger-nail
extended aggressively under the Priest's chin as the
man struggled to lift his head high enough, resorting
to tiptoes in order to avoid a severed jugular.

'It will not happen again my Lord Dagon. You
have my word.' The Priest gulped slowly, trying to
maintain his balance. 'I did not know you had chosen
her.'

Dagon retracted his nail as his expression
became a sneer. 'She is not to be sacrificed you
imbecile, I have a special task I need of her. All you

need to know is she will not bow to you again. Do you understand?'

'Yes my Lord. It shall be as you order.'

Chapter 4

Asherah rolled her eyes and took a long, deep breath that made her nostrils quiver. 'Can you believe the gall of him? His wife! How dare he?' The goddess floated above the temple, her hair drifting behind her as though the wind were blowing.

'He is a dark angel Asherah, cast out for eternity. I doubt he cares who he offends.'

'Anath, you cannot possibly take his side in this?'

'I would not dare sister. Do you want me to cut off his head?' Anath drew her golden sword and presented it to Asherah. 'You have only to ask.' Her lips curled in an almost feral manner.

'For Father's sake Anath, you cannot fix everything with that blade.' Asherah sighed, pushing the still glowing sword toward her sister.

'I am fairly certain I can, but if you are sure?' Anath sheathed the weapon reluctantly.

'Dagon is up to something.' Asherah rubbed her chin and frowned.

'He is always up to something. We are not supposed to meddle Asherah. These are not even your people.' Anath's protest was weak. She wanted nothing more than to break her boredom with a battle and Dagon was always a great source of entertainment.

'But that poor girl. He is taking advantage of her.'

'I am sure she will not be the last. It is the plight of the peasant women in the earthly realm.'

'It is the plight of the wealthy ones too Anath. Father has no idea what Dagon is up to. When the Watchers fell, it left no one to report the dark angel's mischief to Him.'

'He has other matters to deal with Asherah. Moloch has finally shown his hand and war is coming to the heavens.'

'Try not to be so excited. The Prophecy is yet to be fulfilled. The bringer of peace will come and when he does, the heavens will be restored.'

'Yes, but we have a long wait before us and personally, I am happy to bide my time with a battle. So, leave Dagon to do whatever it is Dagon does and let us focus on gaining support for Father here, now, before Moloch brings about a revolt in heaven as well as down there.' Anath released her silver wings, preparing to take flight.

'You go. I will stay sister.'

'Your heart bleeds for them, always Asherah. They have to grow up eventually you know.' Anath secured her shield by her side before gracefully disappearing through the fold of space between Heaven and the world below.

'Now where are you Samson?' The goddess closed her eyes and felt for the essence of the gladiator for God.

The man was a Nazarite, born to serve the Lord with zealous power and serve he did, yet so many had already died at his hand and Asherah often wondered if her father truly understood the fragility of human life.

Asherah found Samson waiting outside the temple of Yahweh. His back was to Dagon's temple, but Delilah would be coming out at any moment. The timing had to be perfect. The goddess could not explain exactly why but somewhere in her spirit she knew these two were destined to meet again. If nothing else, Samson could protect Delilah from Dagon.

It took a moment to focus her energy. Gently she nudged the Nazarite to turn as Delilah leapt through the temple entrance.

Satisfied, Asherah sighed her relief and followed her sister through the Veil of time and space, into the eternal realm.

****

Samson could hardly believe his eyes as the girl jumped the threshold of the temple and almost skipped down the long stone stairs to the busy market square below.

There was a throng of people mingling between the temples, the various taverns and the central garden full of olive trees and flowers.

'Aviv, look! What are the chances of that?' Samson pointed to his precious find.

'By the Creator's blessing, I do not believe it.'

'Us visiting the temple cannot be a coincidence my friend. God is good.'

'Maybe those soldiers sitting in wait were not so foreboding my friend.' Aviv grinned from ear to ear. 'Let us find our coin'

'My coin you mean.'

'Yes, a slip of the tongue, please forgive me.' Aviv bowed theatrically.

'I will think on it.' Samson nudged Aviv. 'Quick, we should keep our eyes on her. She is a swift one.'

The two men watched their thief make her way through the garden, past the pond and on into an alley that ran between the tavern and an outside dining area where patrons sat sipping wine and watching their children play as the sun began to set on a warm day.

'Nice for some.' Aviv nodded at relaxed diners as they moved past.

Samson was too engrossed in following his prey to take notice. More twists and turns brought them to a warren of old white-washed homes and dingy dirty alleys that were barely wide enough to walk down two abreast.

'Not so nice for others.' Aviv finished.

The girl disappeared into a run-down building with an arched doorway, two narrow slits for windows where faded curtains hung and no front door to speak of.

Both men stopped and ducked out of sight while they considered their options.

'You still want to collect your coin?' Aviv ventured, his eyes moving between the ramshackle home and his friend.

'I might have a better idea.' Samson seemed to be pondering, somehow weighing up his choices.

'I know that look Samson. It is not a good look.' Aviv frowned his concern and moved in front of his friend. Samson loomed over Aviv like a giant but that never deterred Aviv from trying to keep the Israelite out of trouble. For someone who upheld the laws of Israel, he had an awfully bad habit of disobeying the laws of every other land.

'Do you think her father will accept my status for her hand?'

Aviv slapped his forehead. 'For the sake of all that is sane. You do recall what happened last time you married a Philistine?'

'Of course I remember. What kind of question is that?' Samson's look was one of genuine offence but Aviv carried on undeterred.

'Well let us just take it a little slower my friend. How about you introduce yourself as a suiter first, possibly even a benefactor; someone who *may* wish to marry the man's daughter?'

Samson seemed to consider Aviv's words and the smaller man began to relax, but as Samson moved toward the home, he was not so sure.

'Was that a yes?' Aviv bounded after his friend. 'I am just checking before we go in there and you are forced to kill another swathe of Philistines to appease your honour.'

'Aviv, I believe I will play this by ear. Let us sound out the girl's father.' Samson grinned with genuine excitement as he walked purposefully toward the adobe hut.

Chapter 5

'Your mother is worried about you Delilah.' Fajer passed a drink of water to his daughter and sat down next to her, sighing softly.

'I am fine father. It has just been a difficult transition.'

Fajer knew Delilah was telling him what she wanted him to hear, but somewhere in his heart he sensed his wife was right. Delilah's time for excuses was over. He needed to act now before it was too late.

'Delilah, you are treading a fine line child.'

'I am not a child! I wish you and mother would stop fussing over me. I am eighteen, old enough to have children, old enough to marry yet you continue to treat me like a child.'

'Yes, of course we do, because you are not yet married. You need a man to care for you, to protect you and to provide for you.' Too late Fajer saw his daughter's posture change. The cup of water flew across the room, slamming hard against the doorframe as a man's head appeared.

Fajer gasped and Delilah frowned at the intrusion.

'I apologise if I am interrupting. I would have knocked, but you do not seem to have a front door.' Samson waited, his gaze drifted to the broken clay cup and the water slowly seeping into the dry dirt floor of the girl's home.

Delilah stiffened as she recognised the big man.

Fajer looked from his daughter to the visitor and a strange look appeared on his features.

'Not an interruption at all. Please, please come in sir.' Fajer jumped to his feet and almost dragged Samson into the small cook room. Samson squeezed past the overly large table and considered the décor. Excessive ornaments seemed to line the home of what was obviously a poor family.

'He is not welcome here father.' Delilah backed away from the cook room, looking as though she might be willing to run at any moment.

'Delilah, your manners.' Fajer frowned to his daughter then turned back to his guest with a sweet smile once more in place. 'To what do we owe the pleasure of your visit?'

Samson had not prepared himself for this meeting. In fact, if truth be told he now really could not think what motivated him to come into the girl's home. He should have simply reported her to the authorities and sent Aviv to retrieve his money.

A cough sounded from the doorway and Samson turned, suddenly recalling Aviv was accompanying him.

'Oh, my goodness. Another visitor.' Fajer turned to his daughter, a question in his eyes that spoke volumes.

'I have no idea who these men are father. Why on earth are you inviting strangers into our home?'

Delilah was looking for an escape, but now with the big man and his friend filling the small room and blocking the exit, she had nowhere left to go except the back of the small building.

Just as she considered an alternative escape through the window in the rear of the sleeping room, her mother moved up from behind her, blocking her final exit. There was nowhere left to run.

Samson watched the girl; she looked panicked for only a moment before her fear turned to anger. He saw her eyes begin to blaze and she drew back her shoulders and took a long, deep breath.

'I have a proposition for you.' Samson spoke before Delilah could reveal her transgressions.

'Come, sit. We do not have much, but what we have we are always happy to share. Is that not true Amariah?'

Delilah's mother pushed her forward, obviously sensing what her father was up to. 'Of course Fajer. Take a seat Delilah and keep these nice men company.'

Delilah's mouth was hanging open as words suddenly escaped her. She numbly took a seat at the far end of the table as far from the big man as she could. Slowly realisation struck. If he was going to reveal her theft, he would have done so already.

'So, where are you young men from?' Amariah made polite conversation as she poured cups of cool water and passed them to the men. 'We have some bread and goats'-cheese, not much mind, but we would be honoured to share it with you.'

Fajer nodded his agreement as Delilah's scowl returned. 'Yes, you look pretty in your fine clothes. Tell us, where are you from?' Delilah locked eyes with Samson as she spoke.

'Let us start with introductions, shall we?' Samson matched Delilah's stare before a grin appeared at the corner of his lips. 'My name is Samson and this is my friend Aviv. We are here in an official capacity really.'

Delilah fought the urge to up and run out the doorway. Both men still occupied that end of the table and she knew they would have her before she could make her escape.

'Oh, such an honour Samson, your reputation precedes you. I had no idea you were in Sorek.' Fajer seemed genuine as he spoke and Amariah's smile widened.

Aviv watched the girl's parents and an unsettled feeling began in his stomach. 'So, you have many lovely possessions. Tell me why your daughter wears rags?'

Samson knew what Aviv was doing. He stomped his foot down on Aviv's from under the table and the man cringed with pain. 'What my friend is trying to say is that I would like to take your daughter with me when I leave. Call it an opportunity to rise above her circumstances.'

'Absolutely not!' Delilah was on her feet now and this conversation had to stop. She just did not know how to make that happen.

'Delilah, sit down. This is not for you to be a part of. This is a conversation for your elders.' Fajer knew the words came out wrong, but it was too late. Delilah had that look on her face that warned everyone she was about to explode.

'How dare you discuss my future like I am some piece of livestock! How dare you!' She stormed from the house knowing that this time, the two men would not attempt to stop her.

She ran and ran until her lungs burned and found herself winding through now darkening streets. She found her way to her hidden gold. After retrieving her life's savings, she went to the only place she knew would be safe.

The Acolyte was preparing the altar for the night's sacrifice. Nearly all the political leaders and wealthy business owners would be in attendance and she knew her window of opportunity was short. 'Kaamill, I need your help.'

The Acolyte saw Delilah and smiled. 'Of course, anything. What do you need?'

'I need to escape Kaamill. My parents plan to marry me off to someone I stole from. He is surely going to beat me after what I did.' Kaamill had never seen Delilah afraid and the excitement of the fear almost made him transform. He forced the one wing that began to bulge at his back to return to its place.

'They would never do anything that was not in your best interests Delilah. I am sure of it. Who is it they wish for you to marry?'

'Someone called Samson.'

'Ah, a powerful man but not known for beating women.'

'How do you know him?' Delilah frowned, suspicion seeping into her bones.

'I have heard of him. An Israelite Judge, killer of many Philistines including his ex-wives' brothers and an entire village.'

'No!'

'Yes, they dishonoured him at the wedding feast and he wiped them all out single-handedly. There would be an enormous reward for anyone who discovered from where his strength came.'

'Really?' Delilah's mind was racing. Such wealth could restore her family to their former position with King Dawsar or even better, it could take them far away to a place where Israelites and Philistines do not even exist and she could marry whoever she wanted to and have children and no one would ever persecute her again.

Kaamill watched the girl carefully. He could feel her fear, but it was abating. Such power within such a tantalising vessel. When this was all over, Delilah would be his.

'You could stay here I guess. I could hide you, but if the priests find you, they might choose you for the next sacrifice. I would hate to see that.'

Delilah forced her mind back to reality. 'I could always lose my innocence to you Kaamill and then they would never sacrifice me.'

'True, but then they would kill me for defiling a virgin of Dagon.'

'Oh Kaamill. What should I do?'

The young Acolyte smiled and embraced Delilah. Her scent was intoxicating and the veil of deception threatened to fall away once more. The dark angel longed to take this young woman, but he would have to wait.

'Can you forestall a marriage and agree to join Samson as his betrothed? Maybe you can find a more suitable husband once you join his ranks in Israel. He is very powerful there. The last Judge of the Hebrew people holds more sway than any King of the Philistines ever has and if you discover the source of his strength, you would be well rewarded.' Dagon smiled at Delilah's obvious understanding.

Chapter 6

Silence befell the little house as Delilah stormed out. No one spoke while Amariah fussed over the table preparing food for her guests. Both Samson and Aviv nodded their thanks as a small wooden platter cracked and beaten was placed before them.

'I am sorry my Lord, she is not always so rash.' Fajer's shoulders slumped as his hopes fell away.

'Nonsense. I like a woman who knows her own mind.'

'You do!' Fajer recovered quickly. 'The ornaments, to answer your friend's question are Delilah's dowry. Yes, they would have purchased her more lavished food, but then she might never have found a suiter without a sizable dowry and that was never going to do.'

Aviv softened his approach suddenly understanding the man's dilemma. Feed his family well or suffer a short discomfort in the hopes of finding his very beautiful daughter a better future. 'I apologise. My comments were made without any understanding and it was rude of me.'

'No, no, you were right to question my choice.'

'Where did you come by such possessions, if you do not mind me asking?' Aviv was curious but careful not to offend.

'I worked with King Dawsar at one time, as his personal advisor. Unfortunately, or possibly fortunately I do not really know which to be honest, but when I discovered the man had some terrible plans in mind for the Hebrew people, my situation became tenuous. You see Delilah is half Hebrew, half Philistine. When I questioned his plans, he banished me. I took all our possessions with us. A blessing when you think about it.'

'What do you mean?' Talk of marriage was suddenly forgotten as Samson put down his cup of water and leant closer to Delilah's father.

'A blessing to be sent away before it was discovered that she was half Hebrew.' Fajer frowned his confusion.

'No, what do you mean about a terrible plan?' Samson leant forward, pushing the food away and focussing his intense gaze on Fajer.

'Oh, I have said too much.' Fajer placed his hand over his mouth and held it there as he realised what he had revealed and to whom.

'Tell him Fajer. Delilah's future may hang on Samson having this knowledge. You said yourself that the King would never take you back now.'

Fajer took a deep breath. 'Yes, yes. The Philistines aim to take away the Judges' power over the Hebrew people. Your power. He plans to make them answer to him and only him.'

'How does he plan on doing that?' Aviv interrupted. 'Samson is the only Judge left and his power is renowned.'

'I do not know. Honestly!'

'If you did, would you tell two Hebrews?' Samson asked without malice.

'I would. You have my word I would. For Delilah, for Amariah, I would do anything.'

****

Asherah watched the Angels of war as they practised their craft. Anath by all appearances seemed gentle enough, but Asherah knew her sister was a formidable fighter. Their sister Astarte sparred with Anath, their long hair tied back and barely visible below polished helmets.

They could not be more different, yet both were breathtaking in their own way. Anath had golden hair, pale skin and a tall lean body, while Astarte was voluptuous by nature with glistening dark hair, almost black eyes and bronze coloured skin.

'Both more beautiful every time I see them.' The sound sent shivers down Asherah's spine but she resisted showing her unease.

'Moloch. How is it that you have not been thrown to the earth with your brethren?'

'Ah sister. As I have told you so many times before. Our father is not as omnipotent as he would like us all to believe. He cannot be or he would have done just that.'

'He is. Father has his plans. He just does not always reveal them to us.'

'True. He does not seem to reveal them to the humans either.' Moloch's laughter sounded hollow as he turned and joined Tannin and Lilith who linked her arms around Moloch's neck and brushed her almost bare breasts against his chest.

As they moved away Asherah sighed in frustration.

'Father why? Why do you allow these Angels to stay here after everything that the fallen have done?'

'Because he loves them Asherah and he does not judge them as we do, no more than he judges the humans as we do.' Asherah turned to the melodic voice of her most reliable friend and mentor.

'Michael! You are not supposed to read my thoughts.' Asherah tried to sound annoyed but she could never hold a scowl with Michael. His soft eyes and inner strength were always there for her.

'Father plays a very long game. You know time does not pass for him as it does for the humans. The war is coming in Heaven, we know it is, but the hope of our future is also the hope of humanity.'

'I know Michael, but I feel powerless.' Michael laughed and stepped forward to take Asherah into his arms. The Goddess wrapped her arms around his waist and buried her head into him. The Archangel stood so much taller than her that she barely reached his midriff.

'You are not meddling again are you Asherah?'

'Of course I am. Father made me this way; you cannot tell me I am supposed to ignore my very nature for a few silly rules. They do not apply to me and you know it.' Asherah pushed away from her mentor and smiled mischievously.

'Well in that case, you might want to take another look at your latest quest. I think it is off target.'

Asherah slapped Michael on the chest for his teasing and frowned. 'You knew all along.'

'Nothing goes unnoticed here Asherah, you should know that by now. Moloch does not see everything, but Father truly does.'

'Well nice of him to talk to you about it. I have not heard a word from him in eons.'

'When you graduate to Archangel you can speak with him more often, but for now, you are in training. Look after my people Asherah. You know I have a soft spot for the Hebrews.'

'I will Michael. I promise.' Asherah hugged the blue-eyed angel before her and snuggled into his embrace as he wrapped his soft silver wings tightly around her.

As they parted, Asherah could see Moloch watching them. He whispered something into Tannin's ear and they both moved away from the gathering.

There was no doubt in Asherah's mind where they were going. Dagon was planning something against the Hebrews and she knew that Samson and Delilah were right in the fallen angel's focus.

As soon as they were out of view and Michael had gone to join the training, Asherah released her wings. The feeling of weightlessness was intoxicating and the sense of peace that touched her spirit as she descended through the Veil of time and space that separated Heaven from Earth never grew old.

If only everyone could know that peace she thought as she descended to the house of Delilah. She watched as the young woman returned to her home. She could feel the presence of Samson within and wondered what had gone astray while she had been away.

It seemed that she would need to stay around to ensure Dagon did not upset her plans. She closed her eyes and focussed on Delilah's thoughts. They were difficult to read. She was confused, angry and frightened—a dangerous combination for anyone but in the short time Asherah had known Delilah, they seemed a more volatile combination for her than anyone Asherah had ever met.

Chapter 7

'Then it is settled. Delilah will come back to Gaza with me. Aviv has a home there where we can stay and I will take care of her.'

Delilah walked through the doorway, overhearing the tail end of the conversation. Her mother gasped, expecting an outburst from her daughter, but instead Delilah just smiled, collected up a clay mug and poured herself a drink of wine that had appeared on their family table since she had left.

'What are we celebrating? I have not seen wine in our home since we left Gaza.' Delilah straddled the bench seat before lifting her leg over without any care for proper etiquette.

Aviv's eyes followed the passage of the beautiful young woman's bare legs as they passed his vision.

'Delilah, Samson has offered to take you back to a more civilised lifestyle. One with the luxury you are accustomed to.' Fajer explained carefully watching his daughter to gauge her thoughts.

'Why Gaza? You are an Israelite Judge. Surely Gaza is not safe for you!'

Samson realised that no one had mentioned he was a Judge before Delilah stormed off. Mistrust lingered in the back of his mind, but he could not look beyond the girl's threadbare clothing. For more than one reason he wanted her out of those garments. He chose to ignore her knowledge. She may have simply asked around before returning to her home. She did not appear to be lacking in intelligence.

'I have work and friends in Gaza. Aviv has a home there and we can help your father find you a suitable husband.'

'So you do not want me for yourself? Delilah raised herself from her seat and leant over to take a piece of cheese and flat bread from in front of Samson. She allowed her top to fall low. Aviv's eyes went straight to her pert breasts but Samson's did not waiver from her stare.

Delilah welcomed the challenge in his eyes and remained leaning over the table as she spoke. 'If you do not intend to bed me, why are you helping me?'

She vaguely heard her mother gasp but Samson only smiled. He was enjoying the girl's fire and she could see it in his steady gaze. 'Let us just say that your father has become a friend and I always look after my friends and their family.'

'So for now I am to be your ward, is that it?'
Delilah allowed the locked gaze to fall and returned to
her seat.

'Something like that. You seem to have strayed
from your upbringing and it is my responsibility to
restore some honour to your name.'

Aviv sensed the tension rising between the pair.
'It really has been lovely meeting you all but Samson,
we must be leaving before first light.'

Samson tore his gaze from Delilah to
acknowledge his friend. 'Yes, quite right. May we
possibly bother you to borrow your daughter for an
hour or so to help us pack before we leave?'

Fajer frowned at the request. 'Why must you
leave under the cover of darkness?'

'Well let us just say that Sorek is teeming with
Philistine soldiers and as we have discussed,
sentiment is changing. Our belongings are still at our
accommodation.'

Delilah laughed loudly. 'You want me to
retrieve them? That is priceless.'

Samson returned the mirth. 'No, there is a
price—five gold and ten silver coins with a handful of
coppers to be exact.' Delilah's face paled as she
nodded her understanding.

****

Her mother had cried as they left the city and Delilah struggled with her decision. She could have stayed, admitted to the thievery and taken her chances. She liked the freedom of her new life. However, she knew now, she was headed for certain servitude. One way or another, either for the Philistines, for the temple of Dagon or for Samson, she was locked into being someone's servant. Her only choice was who was offering her the best option.

'What are you thinking about?' Aviv smiled genuinely as he trotted his tall white gelding up alongside the smaller mountain pony she rode.

'I was daydreaming of nothing in particular.' She lied.

'Samson is a good man, really.' Aviv nodded to his friend who kept his distance for now, leading two pack horses some fifty paces ahead.

'Really?' Delilah pulled the thick shawl the big man had given her just before they left, up around her shoulders. It smelt of sweat and hay, neither of which bothered the young woman. The desert night was cool.

'He carries the fate of the Israelite people on his shoulders.'

'Why are you telling me this?' Delilah's questioning frown was barely visible in what little moon shone in the night sky.

'He wants you Delilah and you know it. He has sacrificed much to be the leader of men, the leader of nations.'

'Oh, my heart bleeds. Did he lose his entire wealth? Did he have his father ridiculed amongst his own people because he had a half-breed for a daughter?'

Aviv's brow creased. He was making a mess of this. 'He lost his wife, his freedom and many of his friends, but no, not his wealth. He still has plenty of that, if that is all that concerns you.'

'I heard he cast her aside, gave her away like a whore to one of his *friends* because she embarrassed him.' Delilah spoke in a mere whisper.

'She did not embarrass him, she betrayed him and he did not *give* her away, she shunned him after he killed her family for their betrayal.'

'It seems betrayal follows him like a curse.'

'You have no idea.' Aviv trotted his horse forward leaving Delilah studying the two men who were leading her toward freedom or captivity. She still could not be sure which.

Chapter 8

'My Lord Dawsar, how lovely to see you again.'

'Dispense with the formalities Kaamill. I pay you for your information, not your flattery.'

The Acolyte bowed reverently but there was something in his manner that disturbed the Philistine King. He rubbed his long, pointed beard and studied the man before him. 'Tell me Kaamill, why are you still an Acolyte at your age?'

Kaamill lifted his hand and waved the question away as insignificant, but the King was undeterred. 'No! Really, why?' Dawsar could not be sure but he thought he saw a look of impatience pass over the features of the Acolyte of Dagon.

'It is by choice my Lord I assure you. I feel no need to become a Priest. I believe I can serve the great Lord Dagon far more effectively if I am not restricted to running His temple.'

The King seemed to think on the answer a moment before nodding his understanding. 'So, what does the Lord Dagon wish of me?'

'He sends his greetings and thanks you for your support in raising the soldiers required in Sorek to drive the Israelite champion from the city. He further wishes to raise your attention to matters concerning the killer of Philistines.'

'Oh, do share your insights Kaamill.'

The Acolyte grinned before he continued. 'The Lord Dagon wants to remove the Israelites of their last remaining Judge. When this is done, they will be without direction, leadership. They will falter and the Philistine nation will rise.'

Dawsar struggled to contain his excitement. 'I am honoured that the Lord Dagon is with me. I live only to serve the god of our nation. If he sees fit to raise my rule to be stronger than any other Philistine King, who am I to object?'

Kaamill rolled his eyes and tried to remain calm. The man was only human and humans were prone to moments of grandeur, unlike the gods who knew they held the power of the universe in their hands. Now the gods had the right to be arrogant.

'Do not get ahead of yourself Lord Dawsar. The Lord Dagon, our god and sovereign wishes our nation to succeed but in order to do so, we must defeat the Israelite champion.'

'Now that will be a feat Kaamill. How on earth are we to kill the gladiator of the Israelites, the champion of Yahweh they call him you know? He is unstoppable in battle and the source of his power is unknown to anyone. He is like the myths of ancient legend. The powers of the gods themselves run through his veins.'

'I assure you, he is not a god my Lord. He is a man and I have a secret weapon who will soon share the source of the warrior's strength with me.'

'In that case, I thank you for your counsel Kaamill. Please, keep me informed.'

The King nodded a dismissal with his head and watched the Acolyte almost sneer at the formality. The reaction confused the King but only for a moment.

Kaamill swallowed the bile rising in his throat and bowed deeply, ensuring the right level of honour was shown the King of the Philistines. He backed out of the antechamber and waited for the door to close before allowing the bile to reach his throat. He snorted and spat the mucus from his mouth, not trying to hide his disdain from the guards who stood beyond the King's chamber.

As the Acolyte made his way through the halls of the palace of Gaza he studied the ancient pillars engraved with symbols as old as he. 'This is a waste brother. The humans are doomed and we should be fighting our war in the heavens, leaving these pathetic beings to figure out their own mess.'

'Be patient brother. We have eternity to succeed.'

'We do not have eternity Moloch. The prophecy is written. The bringer of peace will end us brother.'

'Trust me Dagon. The girl is the one. She will bring about the fall of Israel. I know it.'

'I know she is the one brother, but she is the one I want. She will be mine, you understand!'

'Patience Dagon. There is a reason you are fallen and I am not. Trust me, you are too brash, too impatient. You will have the girl, but first she has a task to fulfil. A purpose that only she can succeed in.'

The Acolyte strode from the palace down the back alley toward the water's edge. As his feet touched the salty liquid his mind cleared instantly and his heart began to slow. His feet glistened in the fading light and scales appeared, layering one on top of another working their way up his legs toward his waist.

'I will be patient brother, but heed my words. There is only so long I will wait to take Delilah as my bride. She will enter the waters of our sea and rule at my side. She will walk upon the land only when I wish it so for she is too beautiful for the men of this world.'

'It will be as you wish brother, but for now, you must allow her to lure Samson to his death.'

The guise of Kaamill faded as Dagon transformed. His tattoos spread out along his chest and arms like a river and instead of his dark wings sprouting from his back, a fish-like tail grew from his feet as they merged into one. The scales continued to ripple along the surface, changing from green, to blue to gold. Dagon took a deep breath and plunged into the warm clear waters of the sea.

The temple was the last place he wished to be today. The smell of the King's conceit was still strong in his nostrils. He longed to wash himself free. His father was deluded if he thought the humans of this earth could ever reach the level of intelligence and honour he expected of them. They were weak and driven by dark needs—the need for power, money, strength and control. They barely worshipped him, a god who sacrificed virgins for their entertainment. How did the Father ever think they would be anything but the wild animals they were?

The Lord of the Philistines swam as deep as he could into the underwater haven he ruled. Here the fish, the whales, the sharks and all the creatures of the sea did his bidding. Here he was truly a Lord. When he walked the earth, the humans only pretended to worship him, sought out his favour for this venture or the next.

'Why do you love them father? I simply do not understand. They are weak and treacherous and sinful, so easily persuaded to murder and rape, to cheat and steal. They are unworthy and we will not give heaven over to them. Never. If I am unworthy, they are even more so.'

Chapter 9

Delilah was growing uncomfortable mounted upon the mare. 'How on earth is this a suitable way for your ward to enter Gaza? Shouldn't I be concealed in a carriage so that suiters can wonder over me?

Samson looked back at the young woman and for a moment wondered what had urged him to bring her to Gaza.

'For a thief, you can be awfully pompous you know.' Samson returned his gaze to the road ahead and ignored Delilah's continued baiting. He smiled as she almost shrieked in fury.

The day was warm and Delilah had dropped her cloak to sit over her mount's rump. Sweat glistened on her chest and neck and the smell of her rose into the midday sun.

'My home is on the outskirts of Gaza. A modest dwelling. We can officially introduce you once you have had time to clean up.' Aviv fought the urge to reach out and touch Delilah's hand. Her eyes were bright and alert, her sweat-soaked tunic had grown see-through and Aviv fought his arousal.

He rode forward to speak with Samson. 'You are right.'

'What do you mean? What are you talking about?'

'You were right. She is not painted up with eyeliner and colours but she is desirable. We need to get her dressed more appropriately before I forget you are courting her.'

'I am not courting her.'

'I thought that was the whole reason she is coming with us?'

'Initially that was my plan, yes, but that was before Fajer told me about the Philistines trying to kill me.'

'So, let me get this straight in my head. You are not going to marry her?'

'Out of all I just said, that is all you got?'

'Well, yes. If you do not want her, I assume you are genuinely taking suiters.'

'No, I am not *taking suiters* you idiot. I'm using her as bait. She has a keen interest in the Dagon temple. She is known to them from before she left the city right up until she worshipped in Sorek.'

'No, no way. That is just not right Samson. You told her father you would take care of her. Find her a husband in exchange for the information he gave you.'

'And I will. But for now, I need her to infiltrate the Philistine temple of Dagon and find out what they are planning. She likes power and money my friend and I aim to give them to her.'

'But she is a virgin. What makes you so sure she won't be their next sacrifice?'

'Well that is easily remedied my friend. She is obviously keen to seduce me. I believe someone has told her who I am. She wants money and power like all women. I will give her what she wants. I will get what I want and we can both have a little excitement along the way.'

'I am not sure that is what her father hoped for Samson.'

'I will keep her alive. I will keep her from being sold as a whore. That is what her father hoped for Aviv.'

Aviv pursed his lips and bit his tongue. If virtually selling herself to get Samson the information he needed, while bedding the warrior was not a whore, Aviv could not be sure what a whore really was.

****

'Did you hear what he just said?' Asherah looked over her shoulder and Anath nodded.

'Of course I heard. I was standing right here. Are you sure you are doing the right thing sister?'

'I am not sure of anything anymore Anath. It has all gone too far. Moloch plotting against the prophecy, Dagon sacrificing virgins for no reason but to prove that humans are unworthy and now Samson is putting Delilah in real danger to save his own skin.'

'Men! Father should drown them at birth.' Anath smiled at the thought. 'But in reality, that would not work at all. Humans would cease to breed and oh wait, that could be a good thing right?'

'No! Of course not.' Asherah looked hard at her sister until she saw the mocking smile on her features. 'Oh stop that Anath. This is serious.'

'It always is with you Asherah. It was serious when the Israelites laid siege upon Jericho. Father was none too happy when you meddled there you know.'

'Not true at all. Both bloodlines had to survive. It was expected of me to intervene. How else were they all to live?' Asherah placed her hands on her hips and jutted her chin out in defence.

'So you are saying father is not strong enough to manage it on his own?'

'No, I am saying he plans well in advance and he knows the players in the game. He knew full well I would never stand by and watch the Israelites kill all the people of Jericho, my people.'

'Have it your way then. What does he *expect* you to do this time?' It was Anath's turn to put her hands on her hips. The goddesses matched each other's stance in defiance.

'I have to do what father would do. Protect the innocent and let the mighty figure it out for themselves.'

Chapter 10

Delilah held her breath as the small group trudged their way up the winding path to the estate high on the hill.

'I thought you said you had a small house in Gaza?' Samson looked accusingly over his shoulder at Aviv.

'I never mentioned the size of the house. I merely said I had a home in Gaza and Jerusalem.'

'You said a *small* holding. In that case, if this is *small*, I cannot wait to see your home in Jerusalem.' Samson tried to wipe the smile from his face. 'All this from a shepherd's income? I think you have been pulling the wool over my eyes for far too long Aviv.'

'It is a long story, one that I do not wish to share right now Samson. Can we get inside and let Delilah rest? It has been a long and hard journey for her.'

Delilah let out the breath she had been holding and smiled appreciatively at Aviv. He was charming, thoughtful and so very lovely but there was no chemistry between them.

She forced that thought from her mind. He was strong and handsome, attentive and obviously wealthy and she needed to find a husband. What was love anyway? She might not have any choice given her circumstances. Samson had ignored her for most the journey which only confused her. One moment she was sure he was intent on bedding her, the next, she was only an inconvenience.

She sighed. 'I am tired Aviv. Thank you for your consideration. What I would give for a warm bath and a change of clothes.' Delilah smiled sweetly but her eyes never left Samson's back.

She knew she had not yet exhausted all other options. She had the temple and the Philistines lined up to support her. As Kaamill had said, finding out Samson's secret could see her set for life, but friends were rare and keeping Aviv close by could save her life should her other tenuous allies prove unreliable.

The trio rode in silence until they reached the gates of the estate. The white stone walls were high and the gates were constructed of strong oak, reinforced with thick ribbons of black metal. Large bolts had been driven deep into the wood and Delilah had to stop herself from touching them as they opened and the small troupe rode through.

A stable boy ran forward and took the reins of Delilah's mare while Samson vaulted down, lead his horse to the boy and gave him a handful of reins including the two pack horses.

Samson's horse nipped at Delilah's mare and the big man grumbled under his breath, the horse rolled its eye, stomped its hoof but obeyed its master.

Samson moved to the mare with his hand outstretched to assist Delilah but the young woman did not make a move to dismount. 'Aviv, do you think you might be of assistance?' Samson looked from his friend to Delilah and frowned as though considering something.

Aviv looked up after dismounting and smiled his charming smile. 'Why of course my lady.' He bowed gallantly. 'Please, allow me to assist you.' Aviv puffed up his chest and strutted between Samson and Delilah.

'She is using you my friend.' Samson whispered to Aviv as he moved past his friend to take Delilah's sandalled foot gently in his hand to rest it on his knee to aid in her dismount.

'Oh I would die a happy man at the hands of such abuse.' Aviv winked over his shoulder. 'A little jealous yet?'

Samson turned on his heel and headed towards the entrance. He had no idea where he was going but steps were steps and they had to lead somewhere.

Delilah watched him take the steps two at a time. He was an unusually big man, but he moved with perfect balance. She was transfixed as his lean body disappeared from her view.

Aviv considered her gaze without resentment, a smile still plastered firmly on his lips.

****

Delilah had never seen anything like it in her life. Not even when her father served the King had she been so royally treated. Two young women fussed over her from both sides. They undressed her, untied her hair, scrubbed her back and rubbed her hair clean.

'I really can do this myself you know.' Delilah tried to protest.

'Yes of course you can my lady but the master of the house gave us strict orders to prepare you.' The older of the two girls spoke with a strange accent. Her skin was dark and her eyes an unusually deep shade of purple. A tattooed ring of symbols circled her left arm and Delilah could not help but find familiarity in them.

'Prepare me for what?'

'It is not for us to say.' The girl with the tattoo answered.

Delilah lowered her head below the surface of the warm water and rinsed the strange liquid from her hair. She felt uncomfortable in the large pond, almost a little frightened as her body tried to float on the surface, the water nearly too deep to stand.

The room was full of steam that rose like soft clouds from the pool. The walls around the pond cascaded water down the edges from three sides and the sound was loud but serene. It was said that waterfalls fell in a similar way but Delilah had never seen one.

As she rose, she was met by the naked form of her helpers. The younger and smaller girl had bronze skin with dark eyes and she kept her eyes downcast. The older woman looked ahead, her eyes taking in Delilah's form unashamedly.

'What are your names?' Delilah spoke, trying to draw attention away from her nakedness as she dropped her breasts below the water level once more.

'We are forbidden from saying my lady.'

'I am not your lady and you are not my servant. Why are you forbidden from saying who you are?

'We have no names now.' The younger of the two girls looked downcast as she spoke. 'We have served this house since we were children, too young to remember our given names.'

'That is horrible. You poor girls. Who did this to you? Aviv?' Delilah twisted her long hair with agitation and squeezed the water out with more aggression than necessary, before tossing it over her shoulder.

'No. Aviv, the master of the house has been kind. We do not work for the master, we do his bidding, but we are not owned by him.' The young girl's eyes grew fearful and she shifted her weight uneasily as she tried to explain.

The thought of being owned made Delilah's blood boil. How could Aviv employ these women when their owner did not even honour them with a name?

'I will speak with Aviv about this.'

'No, please. You do not understand. There is an order to things.' The youngest girl almost begged.

'You will understand though.' The older woman spoke quietly but there was a tone in her voice that sent tingles down Delilah's spine.

'Shhh!' The wide-eyed smaller girl looked around uncomfortably.

'What do you mean I will understand?' Delilah frowned in confusion.

'It is not for us to say my lady. Please, it is time.' The two women left the water and collected a tightly woven shawl. They opened it wide, with one girl on each side and as Delilah left the pool, they wrapped and wiped her body dry.

The sensation was almost erotic and as the servant with the violet eyes wiped her breasts, Delilah almost moaned aloud.

The girl smiled knowingly and placed her thumb gently on Delilah's nipple. The reaction was instant and the servant moved forward, cupping the full and pert breast in her hand, questioning her mistress with her eyes.

Delilah was confused but not stupid. This was no accident. Aviv or Samson were testing her, which one she could not be sure. She nodded her consent and the young woman took her nipple between her lips and kissed it softly at first.

The sensation was like nothing Delilah had ever felt before. The tingling went from her breast to her core and this time she moaned aloud. The second girl licked her finger on her lips and ran it down Delilah's remaining breast, over her belly-button and beyond.

Delilah almost cried out at the touch. Both women gently guided her to a lounge of soft cushions. They each took turns in touching her seductively until Delilah's cries could be heard beyond the walls of her bathing room.

Dagon licked his lips and watched as Delilah arched her back and cried out again. The vision of her was ecstasy and he wanted to take her there and then, but Moloch was right, she had a role to play and as much as it pained him to share her, Delilah would not be his until she had been Samson's.

The dark angel opened his wings and flew up into the sky, satisfied his servants had awoken in her a desire that would not be quenched until she took the Nazarite for herself.

Chapter 11

'Do not be upset my friend. We are friends, right?'

Samson considered his answer and Aviv smiled at the deliberate prolonged deliberation.

'You can answer anytime you like you know?' Aviv jested good-naturedly.

'Yes, we are friends but I told you I wanted Delilah for myself and you have flirted with her the whole journey from Sorek.'

'You said you had changed your mind. That you were more concerned with making a spy out of her than marrying her. You said you would bed her like a whore, so why would I not flirt with her? She is beautiful, more beautiful than any woman and you have been ignoring her, shunning her.'

'I never shunned her.' Samson puffed his chest out defensively.

'Of course you did and now you plan on forcing her to gain knowledge for you, to spy on the Philistines. What will you do when the King or a member of his family take the girl forcefully to their bed?'

'They would not dare.' Samson flexed his biceps as he clenched his fists.

'Think about it Samson. Why not? If they know she is spying for you, they will rape and kill her. If they do not know she is working with you, then they will seduce her or expect her seduction to lead somewhere.'

Samson grunted his confusion and continued to hold his fists firm, his knuckles growing white.

'You are a great warrior but your strategy of espionage is severely lacking. How will you get her into the palace? Under what guise and should someone recognise her as Fajer's daughter, what then?'

'Stop! Just Stop!'

'Marry her and stop the games Samson or someone else will marry her and you will lose her.'

'I thought you considered marriage insane. What were your words? Something about waiting, courting? Well that is what I am doing.'

'No, that is not what you are doing, what you are doing is using Delilah and putting her at great risk.'

The men were interrupted by the courtyard door opening. Two scantily clad women held the doors as

Delilah entered. Aviv almost choked and Samson inhaled audibly.

Delilah was clean of her travel clothing, her oily lank hair and road dust. Instead she had been dressed in fine clothing of purple and silver blue. The flowing sheer fabric fell from her waist in cascades of colour and her bare ankles were adorned with golden chains and dangling tokens that jingled as she walked.

Both men rose from their comfortable seats in unison, both reaching to assist her to make her comfortable.

The young woman giggled softly despite herself and then on hearing her own voice, she suddenly stiffened, realising how childish she sounded.

'Sit down, for goodness sake both of you. Have you never seen a concubine before?' There was a hint of agitation and Samson frowned in confusion.

'You are not a concubine Delilah. I have asked no sexual favours of you. You will be fed and cared for.'

'But?' Delilah saw the lack of confidence in the Israelite's usual expression and knew she had hit a nerve.

'But I do need some help.' Samson considered his words carefully. Aviv was correct. He had no right to put her in danger but if she understood what was at stake, maybe she would be willing to aid in his cause.

Delilah held out her hand and allowed Samson to assist her to a seat, nodding her appreciation. 'Maybe you should serve me something to eat and drink before we discuss our business arrangement?'

'You know for someone so young, you seem to be pretty demanding!' Samson reached for a goblet of wine as he spoke, unable to notice the tension rising in Delilah's posture.

'What Samson means my lady is that for one so young, your wisdom is amazing, breathtaking, as much as your beauty, to be honest.' Aviv held out a platter of dried figs and strange fruits Delilah had never seen. She stared into his eyes for a moment before looking to Samson to judge his reaction.

'See, now Aviv here has manners.'

'No! What Aviv has is a political tongue. I am wondering where he acquired it.' Samson raised an eyebrow with unspoken accusation.

Aviv shuffled his feet nervously as he took his seat again. 'I have a past like all of us Samson. I have some training in diplomacy. I will tell you about it one day.'

'The same way you will tell me how you acquired two *small* holdings I presume!'

'Enough for now *boys*. What do you need help with Samson?' The big man frowned suspiciously at Delilah. 'You did not tell my parents I stole from you and you did aid them by taking another mouth from their home. I agree that I owe you something.'

'You owe me nothing Delilah, really.' Samson filled his cup of wine and took a seat alongside Delilah.

'So you have no ulterior motive for helping me and lying to my father for me?'

'I do, I need your help. Your father shared intelligence with me that I need help to elaborate on.

'You came to my home before my father shared his past with you. You will have to do better than that.'

'I wanted my coin back.'

'And...'

'And nothing, just the coin.'

'Yet you did not accuse me as soon as you saw me. You lie Samson.'

'Enough! Do you want to help me or not?'

The silence grew. Aviv popped food into his mouth to force himself from wading into the conversation. His eyes darted from Delilah to Samson and he could not wipe the grin from his face.

'I will help you, but know this!' Delilah moved forward on her seat and waved her pointed finger in Samson's direction 'Wipe that grin off your face Aviv.' The man responded by raising his eyebrows and pressing his lips together. 'I am helping you,' Delilah returned her gaze to Samson, 'to repay a debt and for that reason alone.'

Samson waited before slowly nodding his understanding. 'When the debt is repaid, I will return you to your parents if I have not found you a worthy husband before then.'

'Agreed!' Delilah held her goblet aloft and waited for the two men to join her in salutation.

'le-Cha-im.' They all responded in unison.

Chapter 12

Delilah wrapped herself in her sheets as she tossed and turned. Her arms flailed around widely and her mind struggled with what it could see.

The dark wings unfolded above the temple of Dagon. The mist rose around the building and red eyes flashed through the thick cloud. Delilah felt herself tied, she looked to both her arms and could feel the cold stone below her body. The sacrificial channels ran with blood, her blood and ……

The scream escaped her lips as Delilah sat bolt upright, sweat running down her back and the darkness of her dream lifted to reveal a room full of soft moonlight.

'*Do no fear Delilah for I am with you.*' The voice was female and Delilah instantly felt at ease until the doors burst open and Samson entered, followed quickly by Aviv.

'Delilah, what happened? Are you alright?' Samson brandished a long wooden club as a weapon and the young woman remembered again how Israelites were forbidden from carrying swords.

'It was just a bad dream.' Delilah felt embarrassed for the fuss. 'I am sorry; my mind must have been lost in worry over our plans. I will be fine.'

Samson moved into the room and waved Aviv away. Unlike Samson, he carried a sword that no one seemed to notice.

'You do not have to do this Delilah. I am sorry. I should not have asked you to. I will find you a husband within a month, if not, I will send you back to your family.'

'No, I want to help Samson. The King dishonoured my father and he deserves to be brought to heel like the wild dog he is. When he exiled my father, he left us destitute. All this began with him.'

Samson smiled and patted the young woman's hand. He forced his vision not to linger on the low-cut night dress, instead he gazed at her strong eyes. He touched her cheek gently. 'Thank you,' was all he said before he rose to leave.

Delilah reached for his hand and with no strength at all, she held the Nazarite at her fingertips. 'No Samson, thank *you*.'

Samson nodded his head and gently pried his hand from the girl's before turning to leave the room.

Delilah watched the moonlight glisten off his muscular back as Samson left her room. She swallowed hard as a tingling sensation began in the pit of her stomach and moved to more sensitive areas.

Throwing herself back onto the bed in frustration, Delilah let out an audible sigh, punched her pillow and rolled over. Sleep eluded her. Instead she considered what tomorrow would bring.

Aviv would escort her to the temple of Dagon and she would begin the journey of embedding herself into the nobility of Philistine society. They all loved to attend the sacrifices at the temple and Delilah knew she could discover more of what the King planned if she made friends amongst the nobles.

The vision of the sacrifice in her dreams returned. She knew it was a risk. In fact, she understood the only way to avoid the altar was to lose her virginity, but how and to whom. Samson did not seem interested in her and Aviv was more than happy to oblige.

She would have to give the illusion that she was no longer pure and that would take some flirting. Aviv could help her, she was sure he would be happy to play along.

****

Asherah had not set foot on the earthly realm in many years but the situation in Gaza was growing desperate. Dagon was invading the young woman's dreams and Asherah knew only one way to stop such an intrusion.

She passed the Veil of protection that hid Heaven from the earth below. As her foot delicately touched down on the soft grass in the courtyard within the walls of Aviv's estate, she gasped from the sensation.

Oh how she had missed the feeling of moist vegetation. The scent of flowers was intoxicating and not for the first time, Asherah was amazed at the power of the Creator of all things.

The perfection of nature, from the bees that spread the pollen from flower to flower to the precious fruit trees that fed humanity. It was all so wondrous. The complexity of birth, the intricacy of new growth, it was all unbelievably magnificent, just as Yahweh was.

He had created her and all her brethren, if only they could have lived in peace. Instead the Watchers had fallen, seduced by just such beauty as Delilah herself.

Now, they wished to wage war in Heaven and on Earth. Dark Angels against the Angels of Light, some hiding amongst the humans, others plotting in the heavens themselves...

She understood they were jealous. The bringing of peace promised salvation to all humanity. The Heavens would no longer be the sole domain of the Angelic and some of her brothers and sisters objected to the idea of sharing. They would do anything to kill out the line of the source of such salvation.

Asherah walked barefoot, touching every bloom that was within her reach. The birds were silently nesting until dawn but she would embrace them once the sun rose. For now, she had to get as close to Delilah as physically possible and stay close enough to protect her from Dagon both in this realm and in her dreams.

Chapter 13

'Time to get up mistress!' The servant fussed over Delilah as the girl tried to focus. The window covers had been ripped away and light was streaming in, hurting Delilah's eyes with every blink.

'Who are you?'

'I am your personal servant child. Get yourself up. You have a big day ahead. The master of the house has told me to make sure you are ready to leave very soon. You have over-slept you know.'

Delilah studied the rounded figure before her. She seemed old, yet there was something spritely about the way she moved that belied her age.

The woman noticed the girl's stare and smiled warmly. 'Aggie, call me Aggie. Now off with that night shirt and on with something suitable. I hear you are heading to the Dagon temple today. You mind yourself there now child. That place is full of darkness.'

Delilah smiled at the old woman's nattering. It reminded her of her mother, especially when it came to discussions about the temple.

'It is not so dark. There are nice people who worship there. I have seen beautiful pictures of gods and goddesses adorning the walls.'

'Yes, yes. I am sure, but there are dangerous people who go there too you know.' As the old woman slipped Delilah's dress on over her head, she waved her hand in circles around the girl's crown. A golden ring of sparkling fire materialised but disappeared almost as quickly.

'There, now that is better. Now you have everything you need.' The woman smiled and stepped back to admire her handiwork.

Delilah stood and moved to the brass mirror in the corner of the room. It was amazing. After the night she had experienced, she was surprised at how neat her hair was and how fresh she looked.

'You are fabulous Aggie. Thank you for your help. I have no idea how you managed this.' Delilah turned in front of her reflection and Aggie could not help but smile at the child-like joy on her face.

'Run along now dear. You have work to do. The master and his big friend are waiting in the large courtyard, down the hall, through the atrium and to your right.'

The halls were long and the home of Aviv was more like a palace fit for a king than the home of the poor shepherd Aviv claimed to be. Delilah was not about to bite the hand that fed her, so she had asked nothing of Aviv but the questions kept springing to her mind. She wondered how much Samson knew.

Delilah was nearly lost in the winding hallways but eventually found her way to a different courtyard from the day before. This one was large, big enough to host a huge dinner party. It was surrounded by palm trees and flowering long grasses. The ground was covered in sparkling sandstone squares and the path was lined with small tufts of grass.

In the centre was a large pool of water, square and shallow with exquisitely coloured stone lining the edges. Past the pond Samson and Aviv waited, talking quietly amongst themselves as they sat on a day-bed, shaded by yet more palm trees.

Delilah resisted the urge to pinch herself and instead settled for a sheepish grin that she failed to gain control of before she reached her companions.

'What is so funny?' Aviv greeted her, standing to assist her to a seat.

'Nothing is funny, I was just smiling at all this grandeur. How is it that you, a Hebrew shepherd can afford such a holding?'

Aviv looked from Samson to Delilah and sighed. 'I guess the truth will come out as soon as I introduce you to the local nobility.'

Samson leant forward, his curiosity piqued. 'Do tell.'

'I do not know if I should Samson. We have been friends a long time you and I. I would not want you to think any less of me.'

'Friendship is not gauged by what you own or do not own Aviv. It changes nothing of our past together. You have bailed me out of trouble more times than I can remember. Please, go on.'

Aviv chuckled before taking a long, slow breath and exhaling. Delilah fiddled with her hands in her lap and began to feel self-conscious for Aviv. He was obviously very nervous in sharing his revelation.

'I am not Hebrew and although I am a shepherd, I am more of an owner of sheep. I guess you would consider me more a merchant.'

'And you let me foot the bill and pay all your gambling debts? You let me, no had me pay for the accommodation, the food and the entertainment wherever we went?' Samson tried not to grow agitated, but it took all his strength to control himself.

'I did not want you to think less of me because I had financial support.'

'Or maybe you have been spying on me all this time for the enemy, for the Philistines? You said you are not Hebrew. What are you Aviv?'

'I *am* your friend Samson, truly, one of the only ones you have. There are many who want you dead. I have never betrayed you Samson. Never!'

Chapter 14

Delilah walked with her arm nestled over Aviv's. He smiled adoringly as they agreed. She needed to appear as his conquest to avoid being chosen as a sacrifice to Dagon.

'Aviv, so good to see you. It has been quite some time since you have graced our threshold. Where on earth have you been?' The Priest was tall, lean and bald. He smiled widely but it never reached his eyes. Delilah shivered and Aviv patted her hand reassuringly.

'Majdi, yes. I have been travelling. You know how much I enjoy immersing myself in different cultures. Speaking of which, I must introduce you to Delilah, my new…friend.'

Majdi smiled knowingly. 'Yes, of course. Your reputation is well known and deserved Aviv. Please enter. Will you be joining us this evening, at the ceremony?'

'You know normally I do not enjoy the spectacle, but Delilah here has a lust for such things. I am sure the nobility would enjoy her company. She is a delightful creature.'

Delilah stiffened at the impertinent discussion. She felt somehow defiled and dirty as Aviv so easily talked in a language that the Priest seemed so much to enjoy.

Aviv squeezed her hand and smiled in her direction as he continued his flippant disregard for her honour. If she did not know better she would have thought Aviv was painting her as a harlot, a whore for hire. Maybe he was?

'Excellent. We will see you after the moon rises this evening.' The Priest beamed with excitement; this time his grin was genuine and Delilah continued to force her emotions to remain in check.

Aviv guided her into the temple. 'Why are we going in?'

'We need to keep up appearances.' Aviv drew her closer, kissing her on the cheek as he whispered. 'Here, let us study the architecture.'

'Why did you make it sound as though I was free to bed any man? I felt violated.' Delilah spoke quietly but there was no mistaking her anger.

'These buildings really are quite marvellous. I often wonder how they move such large stones.' Aviv ignored her question, instead he looked around to ensure no one was listening.

'With slaves.' Delilah grumbled

'If you appear an independently wealthy and confident woman, these men will not risk sacrificing you to Dagon. It will also open up conversation. You are free to decline any advances.'

Delilah patted the man's hand. She knew he meant well. It was really Samson she was angry with. He was no different from the temple he despised so much. She was still a whore, just of a different kind.

****

Samson waited until his friend entered the temple and turned to leave. The idea of encouraging either Aviv or Delilah to stay in such an evil place left a bad taste in the man's mouth, but the need to save the Israelites from anarchy was paramount.

If the last Judge were to die, there would be no one to enforce the Torah, the commandments left by Yahweh to guide his people.

Samson recalled the discussion earlier that morning. It had been heated and at first Samson was angry at Aviv for keeping such a secret; a merchant, the son of a most financially influential man and not an Israelite at all—a Philistine by birth. The news had taken the big warrior's breath away and almost broken his heart.

He had known Aviv since they were young men. They had trained together, shared everything.

There had been no time to fully discuss the lies and Samson had made it perfectly clear the conversation was not over, but Aviv and Delilah needed to leave. It was important they make contact at the temple today. The moon was full tonight and the ritual was sure to take place this evening.

As Samson turned to leave, he almost collided with an Acolyte. He was a tall fellow with a sharp jawline, lined with rather pretentious sideburns. The boy mumbled an apology and went about his business.

Samson had people to visit in Gaza. There was no Israelite temple allowed but that did not stop the underground movement of his people. If the Philistine King was planning to remove him from power and take away what was left of the Israelite's freedom then the Rabbi of Gaza needed to know.

Chapter 15

Delilah froze as the Acolyte entered the temple. Aviv looked at her, sensing her apprehension.

'You know him?'

'I do, from Sorek. He was an Acolyte there. What is he doing here?

'Nothing good I expect.'

Aviv moved to block the boy's view of Delilah but he was too late.

'Delilah. Unbelievable. I thought I would never see you again.'

Aviv leant into Delilah and moved to kiss her neck. She tried to pull away, but the merchant grabbed her by the back of the head and whispered into her. 'Play along.'

Delilah relaxed and allowed Aviv to caress her seductively. She fought the tingling sensation that moved from her neck and down throughout her body.

She feigned shock. 'Kaamill, what are you doing here?'

'I could ask you the same questions and who is your friend?'

Aviv stepped forward. He was a big man, nowhere near as intimidating as Samson but he set an imposing figure to the slim Acolyte. 'You could, but that would require the permission of her benefactor. Now move along lad, before I tell Majdi that you are annoying my friend.'

Kaamill bowed his subservience and moved along, hiding a smirk as he moved away.

'That was just mean. Kaamill has been nothing more than friendly to me the whole time I was close to starving in Sorek.'

'Well you are no longer starving, or in Sorek, so let us stay focussed. Besides, you said he was trouble.'

Delilah was quiet a moment as she considered her position. Kaamill had suggested she discover Samson's secrets and she was undecided if punishing the King or saving her own skin was to be her priority.

Finally she nodded her agreement and took Aviv's arm.

'You smell delicious by the way.' Aviv smiled

'You had best watch yourself Aviv. I think I somehow belong to Samson, although he does not really seem all that excited to possess me.'

Aviv patted her hand again and they moved out of the temple into the sun.

****

Kaamill made his way through the temple, past the altar and around the back to the vestibule. Inside he found Majdi changing his robes and sipping the ceremonial wine.

The man jumped with a start until he realised it was only an Acolyte. 'You do not belong back here boy. Move on before I find something menial to keep you busy all afternoon.' Majdi failed to even notice. He had never seen this particular Acolyte before.

The wings appeared with unfathomable speed and the rush of air they created only angered the Priest. 'I said get….' He turned to see the dark wings open to take up the entire width of the room. He bowed without taking a breath and dropped his chalice, spilling wine onto the stone floor.

'My Lord, please forgive me. I had no idea.'

'That was obvious Majdi. The woman you just met, she is not who she pretends to be.'

'Delilah?'

'Yes, Delilah is the concubine of Samson, or she will be but we need to speed up the process. The man is not human. He should have taken her by now, but he has stalled.'

'I do not understand.' The Priest frowned and tried to retrieve the chalice without being noticed.

'Of course you do not. I have a plan and you will follow it to the letter. Exactly as I say, you understand?'

The Priest abandoned his chalice recovery and wiped his hands on his robes. 'Of course. Of course. Absolutely.'

He listened intently as Dagon outlined his plan.

Chapter 16

The room was dark and the smell of perfume and cologne filled Delilah's nostrils. The fragrance was a mixture of fruity and flowery smells with a few spices mixed in. In the closed-in room it was almost enough to make her eyes water. She resisted the urge to sneeze and wiped her nose as it ran.

'It is an acquired taste.'

'What?'

'The smell of opulence.' Aviv smiled and Delilah stifled a giggle.

She was wrapped in a thick woollen robe the colour of rubies. A hood sat around her shoulders, covering her long plait and half of her face. She had been painted up by Aggie, her cheeks a rosy pink and her eyes lined like an Egyptian queen. Delilah was not comfortable, but the servant insisted she look the part.

Delilah dropped her eyes as the Priest came closer. She had never felt more out of place in her short life. The streets of Sorek felt safer. She did not look anything like the child who left Gaza and she was not afraid of being recognised but with Kaamill present, the situation was tenuous.

'Delilah, a pleasure to see you again. May I borrow your host for just a moment? We have important business to attend to.'

Aviv nodded delicately but Delilah's eyes were already taking on a wild look. 'I have someone who will introduce you to our guests while you wait. Kaamill, this is Delilah.'

Kaamill moved forward and bowed deeply. He maintained the ruse until Majdi was out of hearing. 'What are you doing here Delilah?' Kaamill's tone was strange and Delilah frowned then baulked as the Acolyte reached to take her by the arm.

'I do not understand Kaamill. What do you mean? I am here as a guest.'

'No, you are here as a spy but who you work for is what I am truly interested in.' Delilah tried to pull her arm free of the boy's grasp but he was stronger, far stronger than he looked. She looked over her shoulder as he pulled her away from the throng of people into a darkened room behind the altar.

'Please Kaamill. You are frightening me.'

'You have no idea how frightening I can really be Delilah.'

'You are not making sense Kaamill.'

'Let me make this very clear. Your employer or lover, has he not taken you to his bed yet?' Kaamill went on without waiting. Delilah was squirming and that was exactly how he needed her. 'Samson has asked you to spy on the King and the nobility of Gaza.'

Delilah tried to speak but the words simply would not come out. How could he possibly know? What was he going to do?

'You have a choice. You can aid Dagon, serve him as I suggested you do back in Sorek or you can watch your family perish.'

'I do not understand.'

'Yes, yes. You said that already. You are a smart girl Delilah.' Kaamill was speaking to her as a master would speak to a slave and she began to shiver. 'And if the thought of killing your family does not move you to obey, then you will be sacrificed on the next moon.'

'No. Please, no.' Delilah gasped. 'I will not spy, I will not tell Samson anything.'

'You will have to do better than that Delilah. Samson is strong, stronger than any man known. You will discover his secret Delilah or first your family will die, then you will die.'

'Delilah, there you are.' Aviv rushed towards the girl who looked white and about to faint.'

'I, I.'

'What is wrong, you look like you have seen the walking dead.'

Delilah looked around and Kaamill was gone, disappeared into the thin air. Maybe she had seen a ghost. Maybe Kaamill was never truly there at all.

As if reading her thoughts, a cool wind blew past her face, forcing the hood from her face and sending her into uncontrollable shivers.

'I have to leave.' Delilah did not wait for an answer, instead she rushed from the temple without a backward glance. She did not wait for Aviv. She did not slow her pace. Instead she ran the full ten blocks to Aviv's estate.

She was exhausted from the climb up the hill and her eyes were wild as she made her way into her room. Aggie met her at the door, a look of concern flooding her face.

'What ever happened child?'

'Nothing. Nothing at all.' All she could think of was how she was to reveal Samson's secret and save her family before the next full moon.

Chapter 17

'What do you mean she left?' Samson sat with Aviv in the courtyard where he had waited for the ritual to be complete.

'She left. She was scared Samson. Something frightened the life out of her. She ran all the way back here and locked herself in her room.'

'This is all wrong Aviv. First I find out you are not who you say you are and now Delilah refuses to do what we need.'

'Stop it Samson.'

'Stop what?

'Being a selfish ass.'

'I am not an ass, I am a Nazarite, sworn to serve Yahweh no matter the consequences.'

'That is excellent. Get me or Delilah killed but stay true to your code soldier. What kind of god demands that of anyone?'

'Do not blaspheme my God.

'It is only blasphemy if I believe and I do not believe in a god who wants to see Delilah's death. I have had enough Samson. If you wish to force her to die for you, then you can do it yourself.'

Aviv stood and made to leave.

'Do not walk away from me Aviv.'

'This is my home Samson. I will do as I please. You hold no power in my house except your strength and you can kill me or beat me, but I will not send Delilah back to that place.'

Samson put his face into his hands and ignored his friend as he left. Delilah was driving him insane. He needed to serve Yahweh but all he could think of was the girl. Every waking moment and even his dreams were obsessed with her.

The Nazarite rose from his seat and took the long walk down the halls until he reached Delilah's room. He went to knock, but thought better of it.

He laid his face upon the heavily carved wooden door and brushed his hand against the handle, still he could not make himself open the door or knock on it. How was she doing this to him?

****

Asherah's body lay on her divan in her room, but her spirit floated above Delilah, focussed on protecting her. She could see Samson leaning against the door but he would not enter.

The goddess could not say exactly why, but she knew Samson needed Delilah. Yahweh had sworn him to service, but the man was missing something, something that only Delilah could give him.

'You are meddling again Asherah.'

'And you should not be in this realm Moloch. You are forbidden.' Asherah returned to her body and took flight. She needed to draw her adversary away from both Samson and Delilah.

The angel followed her into the Veil, his hands on his hips and his lips set in a scowl.

'I know you think my path is against father, but it is not. It is to preserve everything that he created for us.'

'No Moloch. Your path is about jealously and greed. You wish to keep immortality for the angelic only and father has promised it to all of humanity if they so choose.'

'You are aiding Dagon you know. He wants Samson and Delilah together. He has great plans for them both.'

'They are to be together, but not for Dagon's sake. I have seen further Moloch. Unlike you, I am always focussed on the distant future and there is more to this chapter than what happens to Samson or even Delilah in this reality.'

'You speak of other realms.'

'No, I speak of possibilities Moloch. The book is already written. There is nothing new under the sun. Yahweh has already ordained it.'

'Your blind obedience is childish Asherah.'

'And your rebellion is adolescent. We are all children to our father Moloch and we can all only do what we believe is right.'

Moloch waved his hand and spun himself out of existence.

'You always run away when you are losing a debate Moloch. As I said, adolescent.'

Asherah did not hear his growl but she felt it, deep in her chest. She smiled and chuckled quietly to herself.

****

Delilah tossed and turned.

The blood was running from her wrists, into the channels and down to the floor. At the base of the altar, Samson was tied, his beautiful hair cut short, his eyes gone, his body covered in welts and puss.

'No!' Delilah screamed aloud but did not wake.

The wings were black as charcoal but the face was familiar. Delilah tried desperately to focus on the features but the figure only laughed loudly. 'You know who I am Delilah. We are old friends. You will be mine. I will take you as my own. I will die if you do not obey. But if you obey, you will be my queen.'

'No, No. Please. No!'

The door exploded into splinters that flew through the air like arrows. Delilah tossed about in a ball of sweat, wrapped in her sheets that were now tied around her like ropes. Her eyes remained closed, her face creased in what looked like pain.

Samson ran to her side, shaking her gently. 'Delilah, it is me, Samson. Wake up.'

Aggie appeared in the doorway.

'Get cold water.' Samson screamed to the servant who ignored him. Instead she strode into the room like she owned it and placed her hands on the girl's forehead.

'It is you who must get the water Samson. She is running a fever. I can look after her.'

Samson made to argue but there was something in the woman's stare that warned him against it. He was no healer, maybe she was right. Samson stood and left the room at a jog.

'I am sorry my dear. I should have known Moloch was only distracting me. Dagon has you now but not for long. I will bring you back.'

Chapter 18

Samson held Delilah's hand and changed the cool water compress on her forehead every time it grew warm. He begged Yahweh to save her. He prayed endlessly without words as he kissed her hand and asked for her forgiveness.

It was his fault she was in danger. He did not understand it. Aggie said it was some sort of evil, something she had brought back from the temple. He did not doubt the old woman. Dagon's temple had left him with a sense of unease and he knew there were spirits that opposed his god, but why attack Delilah?

He swore in that moment that he would tear down Dagon's temple. The god of the Philistines would know Yahweh's might... for God, for Israel and for Delilah. The temple of Dagon would fall.

****

He was touching her all over. She felt hot and cold all at the same time. The dark wings enfolded about her and she could feel hands on every part of her naked body. They clawed at her, touched her in a way that aroused her and disgusted her in the same breath.

The dark angel smiled but still she could not see his face. His tongue was long and as black as his wings. She felt its rough surface drag along her neck and as she turned away, he grabbed her chin viciously and pulled it back.

'You will give me Samson. You will tell me his secret and he will die.'

'Time to leave Dagon. She is not yours to contain. She is the vessel of Yahweh and she will not do your bidding.

'It is foretold Asherah. She will. There is nothing you can do to stop it.'

Asherah shook her head. She knew the vision of which Dagon spoke and it had many possible outcomes. 'We will see brother. We will see.'

Delilah shook her head. There were voices speaking into her mind from everywhere. She tried to understand them but they were hissing now.

'Come to me Delilah. Samson is waiting. Stay strong. Follow my voice. Come back to us.'

'That is the way Delilah.' Aggie's voice was raspy but there was something too familiar about it. 'Samson is here. Samson, she is awake.'

The Nazarite was asleep with his head leaning on Delilah's bed. He woke with a start and reached for Delilah's hand.

'I am sorry. This was all my fault.' He begged with his voice unusually quiet.

'How is this your fault?' Delilah could barely speak. 'Water! Please.'

Aggie held a cup to Samson who lifted the girl's head from the pillow and gently dripped water to her parched mouth.

'The temple will fall Delilah. I vow it to you.'

'I do not understand.'

'Neither do I, but Aggie here seems more knowledgeable on these things. While you slept, or dreamt or whatever it was you were doing you were actually being attacked by the dark god Dagon.'

'How? How could you know this?' Delilah looked to Aggie for confirmation.

'I am a healer of sorts. I can sense these things. Besides, you screamed the dark god's name while you tossed and turned.' Aggie smiled reassuringly, yet Delilah remained apprehensive.

'You can leave her now Samson. She needs her rest.' The Nazarite made to protest but Aggie frowned and nodded to the door.

Delilah smiled a tired smile as he left. 'I am fairly certain the big man is unaccustomed to being ordered about.'

'I think you may be correct in your assumptions but contrary to his own belief, he is not in charge of this, Yahweh is.'

'What do you know of Yahweh? I only know the stories my mother used to tell me.'

'I know he loves us all, Philistine or Israelite.' *Angel or Human,* she wanted to say but Delilah was never to know who Dagon really was, or who she was for that matter. 'I know he wants peace in Heaven and on Earth and there are stories amongst your mother's people that speak of a bringer of just such a peace, but that is a story for another day. You need to get some rest.'

'I cannot sleep Aggie. My dreams were troubled.'

'Here, drink this.' Aggie handed a small vial of liquid to Delilah. 'It will keep your dreams happy and carefree.' Aggie smiled and Delilah took the potion from her hands. It smelt sweet and spicy.

'How long did Samson watch me? Delilah laid back on the bed and drew the covers up around her.

'Every moment Delilah. He did not leave your side.'

Delilah shivered and smiled at Aggie. The thought of Samson caring filled her with a sense of comfort but she was still afraid.

'Will you stay while I fall a sleep?'

'Of course child. I will stay as long as you need me.' Aggie sat on the side of the bed and ran her fingers through Delilah's hair before patting her covers down and gently rubbing her arm.

 **Chapter 19**

'Do you think the girl will discover his secret?' Dawsar paced around his antechamber, his hands gripped together behind his back as his robes billowed behind him.

Kaamill bowed deeply and forced himself to remain so for the respectable amount of time. 'Yes of course my Lord. She has much to lose if she does not.'

'Is she close enough to him yet? Has he taken her to his bed?'

'Problems that do not concern you my Lord. You will have the secret to Samson's strength before the next full moon.'

'What if there is no secret? What if he is simply a very strong man?'

Kaamill laughed aloud and quickly wiped the smirk from his face. 'No man can be as strong as Samson without the power of the immortal realm my Lord. He is a Nazarite, protected by Yahweh himself.'

'Yahweh is a myth, a god manifested by old women to stop Philistine men from waging war against the Israelites. Ever since they left Egypt they have been a thorn in our side. First the Canaanites, now us.'

Kaamill did not correct the King. Yahweh was not a myth but admitting it aloud left a bad taste in his mouth. Yahweh was the father of all creation and if he told Dawsar that it was not a myth, that it was fact, it would leave their respect for Dagon depleted. Who would support a demi-god when the said demi-god's father was pulling the strings?

'Dagon will bring Samson to heel my Lord. Last night's sacrifice was precious but we may need to bring another before the next full moon to strengthen the mighty Dagon's power against the Nazarite.'

'Very well Kaamill. I will leave it to you to find the chosen.'

'You do me great honour my Lord. I have the perfect choice in mind.' Kaamill bowed and left the King's chambers to make the arrangements.

****

Delilah felt like she had slept for a month. Her entire body ached, even her fingers hurt when she moved them. Aggie had explained that trauma could do such a thing and no one understood exactly what she had endured at the temple.

'I told you it is a dark place.' Delilah chuckled at the memory of Aggie's shaking finger and frowning reminder.

'You have no idea how dark Aggie.' Delilah spoke the words aloud as she stepped into the steaming hot water of the pond.

Her original companions had lessened to only one since that first visit. The girl with the violet eyes and dark skin with tattoos had become her personal servant.

'May I massage your muscles?' Ebony asked as she begun kneading Delilah's shoulders.

Delilah answered with a moan and the girl forced her thumbs deeper into the soft tissue of the young woman's shoulders. The heat of the water and the rubbing of the muscles soon relaxed her and she broke free of Ebony's careful attention to glide through the water on her back.

'Where did your friend go Ebony?' Delilah asked, suddenly curious about her missing companion.

'She works at the temple sometimes.'

'Which temple?' Delilah asked suddenly feeling apprehensive.

'Dagon's. It is the only accepted temple in Gaza. The others are frowned upon. If you visit the other temples, you might get murdered, your wife raped or have your entire savings taken from you.'

'That is terrible.' Delilah swam back over to her new friend.

'It is an unwritten law imposed by the King. All tributes must go to Dagon, even the virgin sacrifices. No burnt offerings to any other gods.'

Ebony rarely talked of such matters but the bathing room was too noisy with the running water to be overheard and she knew Delilah was always afforded space. Aggie, the new servant ensured it. The men were allowed nowhere near the girl while she bathed.

'So then, you are aware of the sacrifices?' Delilah grew excited with a chance to gain some knowledge.

'Yes, of course. It is an honour to be chosen.'

'An honour to be killed, murdered and have your blood spilled down the channels for some god to feast upon? You cannot possibly really believe that?'

Ebony suddenly felt unsure of their privacy. She looked over her shoulder and studied the large stone room carefully. The corners were full of potted palm trees but they were too small for anyone to hide behind.

'I am a virgin still mistress. I work quietly and try not to raise too much attention. I try not to have opinions on matters of politics or religion.'

Delilah nodded her understanding and ducked her head below the water. Her thick hair took hours to dry but every minute was worth it just to feel the water all over her entire body.

****

'Thank you for abandoning your crazy ideas about having Delilah spy for you.' Aviv was not even short of breath as he started his second lap around his estate, Samson joining in on the run.

The crushed pebbles ground beneath their sandalled feet but the surface was remarkably flat and Samson marvelled at the ingenuity.

'What is this pebble called?'

'Crushed Crystal. It sparkles like a jewel in the sunlight. Very durable, it lasts season after season.'

'Where did you come by it?'

'It is found more commonly across the sea. I told you, I am a merchant. I take minerals, spices, anything of value including sheep and move it from one place to the next to sell it. The further you move something, the more people pay because it is rare, something they have never seen before.

Crystal is such a thing. The Philistine King has spent a fortune on having it added to his training ground. His soldiers train on it every day.' Aviv seemed happy with his entrepreneurial pursuits but Samson was not so sure.

'So you aid my enemy with better training opportunities, just so you can make a fortune?'

'I offered it to the Israelites first. They had no interest in it. Besides, you are not supposed to have soldiers, remember, not even weapons area allowed amongst your people now.'

'You say my people. Who are your people then Aviv?' Samson felt like he needed to start from the beginning with the man he thought he knew so well.

'I have no people Samson, but you are my friend and I will do whatever you ask of me, except put Delilah in harm's way.'

Samson waited a moment, understanding slowly seeping in. Aviv cared deeply for Delilah but there was no doubt in the Nazarite's mind that his friend had no intention of acting upon his feelings.

'I think I will visit the King.'

Aviv stopped running and stared at his friend for some time before responding. 'Do you need me to introduce you?

'I was hoping you would offer my friend.'

'What do you intend to say?

'I will ask him about his plan to kill me and see what he says.'

'Just like that?'

'Just like that!' Samson grinned and took off at a fast pace back toward the estate.

 **Chapter 20**

Samson stopped in his tracks as he made his way back from his run. Delilah was lying upon the divan in the courtyard. Her long hair lay loosely over her shoulders, drying in the dappled sunlight that made its way through the swaying palm trees.

He had avoided her since her night of delirium, feeling all too responsible for her fear and pain. Now the mere sight of her took his breath away. She wore an azure-blue gown that hung low at the front. Her wet hair had left a mark on the top, making is almost sheer over her right breast.

Thoughts of moving on were dashed as Delilah looked up and saw him staring. She smiled and her eyes sparkled mischievously as though she had known what he had been thinking.

She did not call out, instead she waved at him and beckoned him with her hand. Samson looked around to see if Aggie were close by. The servant was never more than a few paces from the girl since the temple incident.

'Samson, I have been waiting to thank you. Wherever have you been?' She patted the divan next to her, swinging her legs around to make room.

Samson looked over his shoulder nervously. Her manner was unusual, almost out of character. 'Are you well?' He asked frowning, but taking his seat by her side.

Delilah surprised him as she replaced her legs upon the divan where they had been before, now directly over the Nazarite's lap.

'I am fine Samson. Much better now that I have caught up on some rest.'

'Delilah, have you taken something?' If he did not know better he could have sworn she were euphoric.

'Oh Samson, it is alright. I like it here in Gaza you know. It is a very nice place.' Delilah giggled and moved to sit straddled across Samson's lap. The room was floating in the most peculiar way and all she could think about was that first bath after she had met Ebony and her friend.

She cupped Samson's face in her hands and kissed him firmly on the lips. He struggled only a little, trying hard not to hurt her.

'Delilah, this is not what you really want. Is it?'

The girl's response was to begin undoing the Nazarite's shirt while kissing him more passionately. Samson knew now she was under the influence of Opium or something similar. Aviv said he traded in anything rare or of high value and nothing fetched more coin than such a drug.

Samson gave in to the kiss and wrapped his arms around the slim waist and hips of the young woman he had desired the moment he had met her. She rolled her hips on his lap and smiled when his body answered her call.

'Are you sure this is what you want Delilah?' Drugs always brought out the true passion of the user. Delilah must want him, of this he was sure, but why? The question niggled at his mind.

It was a fight he was losing, something the Nazarite was unfamiliar with. The battles he had won, the men he had killed were all nothing compared to this struggle. He wanted her and she wanted him, what was the issue?

'Delilah. I want this, really I do, but you need to take this slow.' Delilah kissed him again, biting his lip and licking his tongue with hers. He moaned with pure agony as he held her to him one more time, smothering her mouth with his own, forcing her hips down firmly until he finally released her and physically lifted her to her feet as he rose.

'You need more time Delilah.' He placed her carefully on the divan as though she weighed no more than a feather and left the courtyard without a backward glance.

Delilah sighed and laid back on the divan. 'I tried Dagon, I tried,' was all she said before she passed out on top of the soft cushions, with the speckled sunlight filtered through the palms above, amongst the scented blooms that lingered in the air.

Her mind drifted and with the mere mention of the dark Angel's name. Delilah found his face this time. The face of Kaamill, twisted and distorted as it was that night at the temple. The image faded and Delilah opened her eyes just a sliver to see Aggie striding into the courtyard, waving her hand in circles that sparkled like gold dust in the moonlight.

****

'Who is here?'

'The merchant Aviv and a friend my Lord.' The guard bowed and waited for instructions.

Dawsar knew Aviv had only one friend. He wrung his hands, rubbed his sweating forehead and chewing his bottom lip as he contemplated why Aviv would bring Samson here, to the palace, of all places.

'Show them in then. Do not leave my guests waiting.'

Aviv walked through the door first. A huge bulk of muscle trailed behind him and Dawsar swallowed hard, cleared his throat cautiously before speaking.

'Ah, Aviv, what morsel do you bring me this time?'

Aviv bowed graciously. Samson failed to move. The King challenged him with his eyes and the Nazarite held his gaze for a moment before dropping his eyes and tipped his head just enough to acknowledge his enemy.

'I have many new products to share with you my Lord but for now I was asked to act as an envoy of sorts. I hope you understand. The pay was generous and you know my fealty lies with coin.' Aviv smiled and bowed graciously.

Samson was not buying it for a moment. Aviv might not be the man he once thought he was but he was not as driven by wealth as he would have these Philistines believe.

The Nazarite knew that Aviv's introduction carried with it a great risk to his friend and he was beginning to truly appreciate him.

'Of course Aviv, as long as you do not commit treason against the crown, then all is good. If I am not mistaken, your friend here is Samson the Nazarite.'

'You are one hundred percent correct my Lord Dawsar. Samson, meet King Dawsar of the Philistines.' Aviv leant forward, his hand placed by his lips as if to shield Samson from hearing, 'He does not exactly bow down before kings my Lord. Please forgive his Israelite ways.'

The King chuckled good-naturedly but it was forced and Samson smiled at the discomfort.

'I hear you plan on killing the last Judge of my people Dawsar. Since I am the only one left, I thought I would save you the trouble of looking for me.'

'Straight to the point I see Samson. Maybe you could have eased into that one?' Aviv backed away carefully, making room for his friend to move forward.

'Do I need to call for the guards Nazarite?' The King's voice waivered only a little. Samson was impressed.

'That depends.'

'On what?'

'If you want to die here today. You know your guards would have no hope of beating me.'

'You threaten me? In my own home?'

'This is not your home. It is on loan from your people and you are not taking good care of it *King.*

Try to kill me, many of your men will die and when they fail, I will hunt you down myself. I have been known to tear a man's limbs clear off his body you know. Is that not true Aviv?'

Aviv nodded, but kept his distance. 'You will never sell so much as a trinket in Gaza again Aviv.' The King made eye contact and sneered.

'Oh I doubt that my Lord. You see many of your most loyal subjects, especially the wealthy ones who donate to your cause so generously, have formed a nasty, rather dependent habit. Well it just so happens I control the Opium trade in these parts, so best of luck banning me from Gaza.'

Samson stepped forward toward the King. The guards at the door advanced, their swords raised and ready to attack. 'Tell your men to stand down. I am not in the mood to fight today.'

'You have threatened me Samson and you are known to these men already.'

'The decision is yours Dawsar.' It took only a heartbeat before the decision was no longer the King's to make. The younger of the two soldiers stepped forward and lunged his spear at Samson. He stepped sideways, lifted the spear with the soldier still attached and threw them both against the wall. The sound was sickening.

'I can do this all day Dawsar, I suggest you call your men off.' The second soldier heard the crack of his friend's neck against the stone and reacted without thought. He dropped his spear and drew his sword, circling Samson as he spun the weapon theatrically over his wrist.

'I am unarmed; you would attack an unarmed man in the King's own court? What kind of diplomacy is this?' Samson mocked as the man rushed forward.

He was not well balanced but it mattered not to the Nazarite. He took the clumsy sword blow on his leather bracer and wrapped his arm around the soldier's sword arm. He grasped the man's elbow in his huge hand and lifted, taking the arm and sword with him. The crack of the elbow, then the shoulder joint was audible and the King clambered up onto his dais, calling for more guards.

'Now that was a mistake Dawsar. I told you I meant you no harm so long as you left me and my people alone. Now look what you have done.'

Four more men entered the King's antechamber and surveyed the scene quickly. Aviv held up his hands and stepped aside, not wanting to fight without a weapon.

All four soldiers ran at Samson and the close quarters made it impossible for them to use their weapons. Instead they leaped upon his back like desert cats.

One wrapped his arm around the Nazarite, trying to secure a choke-hold. Another kicked at his leg, taking it momentarily out from under him. As he fell to one knee, the soldiers followed him down, each holding on to a piece of the big man.

There was a moment of stillness, where the King held his breath and Aviv chuckled quietly to himself. The silence was shattered as four grown men, fully clad in armour flew into the air in various directions before coming to an abrupt halt.

'Enough! I am leaving. Dispel your plans Dawsar. Leave my people alone and do not attempt to harass me or you will see my smiling face again. Do we understand each other?'

Dawsar was crouched on his velour throne, his legs pulled up under his robe to somehow make himself disappear. He nodded and Aviv slapped Samson on the back.

As they left the room two more guards appeared, looked to their King, to the men strewn around the room and back to Samson and Aviv before stepping back to make way for both men to leave unmolested.

 **Chapter 21**

Samson and Aviv were still smiling and joking as they strode into Aviv's estate. Aviv stopped at the entrance and Samson turned to follow his friend's gaze.

The right hand front gate hung from only one hinge, while the other lay flat on the ground, chariot marks over the thick wooden structure. Both men ran without thinking, leaping the fallen mess in one bound, landing in fighting stance, their eyes alert, every muscle taut with adrenalin.

A moan from their left brought them to one of Aviv's men, slumped down on the ground, his nose broken, his eyes swollen closed from a huge lump forming between his eyebrows. 'Marcus, what happened?'

'Ah Sir. Thank the goddess you are here. There were too many.'

'Too many what Marcus? We need to know, are they still here?'

The soldier shook his head. 'No Sir. They took the girl.'

'Delilah? Who, why, where did they take her?' Samson moved forward, shaking the nearly unconscious man vigorously.

'Easy Samson. He is no good to us dead. Answer him Marcus.' Aviv held his hand over Samson's forearm, begging him wordlessly not to break anymore of his soldier than he could already see damaged.

'Not that girl Sir. The servant, her, you know her…' The man seemed lost for an explanation but both Aviv and Samson realised who he meant.

'Who took her and where is Delilah?' Samson let go of the soldier and stood with his hands on his hips awaiting an answer.

'They took her to the temple. The Priests of the temple came for her. Said she was to be sacrificed. The Mistress was so upset. We fought as hard as we could Sir but there were too many.'

'Get yourself cleaned up. I will need a full report later Marcus. Where are Delilah and her maid?'

'In the courtyard, Sir.' Marcus was still groggy, but he knew he needed to give Aviv as much information as possible. 'You are not going to believe it when you see it. That woman fought like a lion!'

Both men ran as fast as they could toward the largest courtyard. It was Delilah's favourite place to rest and so far, after what had happened, rest was all she was getting.

No trips to the markets, no visits to food stalls or even a walk to the nearby royal parklands. She had stayed confined by choice, too afraid to leave the tall walls and guarded estate.

As they approached the courtyard, they slowed their pace. Aviv guffawed and Samson simply let out a low whistle. At least twenty armed men were unconscious on the ground and none of them Aviv's.

His men were all tending to the wounded. Aggie was running around with bandages. Delilah sat huddled on her divan, her knees tucked up under her dress, her eyes wide with tear stains down her cheeks.

Samson ran to her, but she hardly recognised his presence. 'What is going on here?'

Everyone stopped at the sound of the Nazarite's booming voice. 'What Samson is trying to say is, well done men. Looks like you put up a tremendous fight.'

'This was not us Sir. This was her.' The soldier nodded to the now catatonic Delilah curled up on the divan. 'We took time to get here most of us Sir and we saw Dagon's temple Priests dragging the girl out of the courtyard by her hair. The Mistress here, she went all berserk.'

'Yes, yes.' Aggie interrupted. 'She was simply overcome with fear.' Aggie felt guilty having done what had to be done to keep Delilah safe. All she could hope was that Delilah was not permanently affected by the experience.

Moving her essence into Delilah's body seemed the only possible solution to Dagon's attack. If she had used her power any other way, the questions would have been endless.

'But the Mistress, she was possessed Sir. That's what it looked like anyway.'

Samson looked to Aggie for clarification. 'I will look after her Samson.'

'Not until you have explained what is going on. This is something that I could do, but not Delilah.'

'Well maybe Yahweh blessed her with power to combat these foul creatures of darkness.' Aggie swept her hand around the courtyard full of fallen men for emphasis. 'They took her friend Samson. This discussion will have to wait.' Aggie nodded to Delilah still curled up like a baby.

Samson turned to look at Delilah again. She was still staring into nothingness. He bent down and lifted her gently with little effort. He carried her back to her room and placed her on the bed. Aggie moved in and shooed him away, covering the girl with a soft duvet and soothing her with words the Nazarite did not understand.

Samson closed the door and Aggie gently gripped Delilah's face, her fingers rubbing the girl's temples as her eyes closed. 'Sleep well child. I have a feeling Dagon is going to be sorry he took your friend.'

****

The scene replayed in Delilah's mind repeatedly, but she struggled to make sense of it. She had been sitting talking quietly with Ebony when the men had stormed the Estate. Aggie had been picking vegetables for the dining table and Ebony had just begun to braid Delilah's hair.

Everything happened so quickly. One second she was frozen in fear, the next she felt nothing but rage spewing up from the pit of her stomach like a volcanic eruption.

The next few moments were a blur. She could see, but not clearly. Her thoughts were muddled but she could still recall what she saw. The Priest, Majdi, had forced his way between the two girls and grabbed Ebony by the hair. 'She comes with us.'

Delilah remembered screaming at the Priest to let her go before the bald man bent forward and spoke quietly for only her ears. 'You have a task to perform my dear and Kaamill insists you do it quickly. Just in case you have forgotten, he is claiming your little friend here. She will die as a reminder to you to do as you are told. After her, will come your family if you do not obey.'

It was at this point that Delilah's delirium returned. She saw men flying in all directions but felt nothing, as though a high yet invisible wall had been erected around her mind.

Delilah woke up to a darkened room. Aggie moved to her side almost immediately. 'Are you alright child?'

'I am better than alright Aggie. I need your help though.' Delilah's tone was determined and Aggie smiled.

'Anything my dear. What do you need?'

Chapter 22

Samson never dreamed, so when he woke up sweating, the memory of hot irons burning his eyes and the temple of Dagon crashing to pieces around him he knew it was a prophecy he had seen.

He would need time to fully interpret the message, but it was clear he would endure great pain but he smiled as he realised that Dagon would pay. He had asked for retribution against the temple of Dagon and now he would have it.

The Nazarite rose from his bed and walked to the bowl of water on his side table. The bronze mirror hung lopsided above the water and Samson looked at its reflection before splashing his face and wiping it with a soft cloth.

He removed the headband from his brow and placed it alongside the bowl. He ran his fingers through his hair before picking up a brush and began to free the long locks of knots and debris. It had been too long since he had cleansed his hair, a ritual demanded of his Nazarite pledge. Yahweh had given him great strength but in return, he had promised to never cut even a strand of it from his head.

It reached his backside now and as much as he preferred to leave it loose and free, the elements were harsh on it—the wind whipping through it, the sun beating down upon it—tying it back was the only solution. After removing all the tangles, the warrior who had pledged his strength to the god of Israel replaced the band around his head and left his room.

As he opened his door he saw Aggie move past toward the cook-room. There was something not right about that woman. It was nothing sinister, but she seemed to handle herself in a way that belied her age. There was a sparkle in her eyes seldom seen in the elderly and Samson often puzzled over it.

He shook his head and moved in the opposite direction toward Delilah's rooms. He smiled as he knew how agitated Aggie would be when she found him there without her.

Samson knocked gently but there was no answer. The Nazarite frowned and knocked again. Frustrated he opened the door to find Delilah's bed made and her missing.

He stormed toward the cook-house to find Aggie. Instead, he found Delilah, packing a bag and motioning Aggie out the door in the opposite direction.

'Where are you going?' Samson demanded as he moved to bar the way.

'I am going to the market. Aggie and I need supplies.' Delilah was confident and strong. Back to how she had been when first they had met. Samson creased his brow and Delilah giggled good-naturedly.

'But you were...' Samson looked behind himself, back toward Delilah's room. 'You were unconscious, in shock. I do not understand.'

Delilah moved forward confidently and kissed the big man on the cheek. 'Well I am none of those things now. You can join us if you please, but it will only be boring market day errands.'

Samson touched his cheek where Delilah's warm breath lingered. 'No, I will find Aviv and we will train his men. They say you beat all those men on your own. They should be ashamed.'

'Why? I have heard you would have taken a hundred more with ease.'

Samson's eyes narrowed. 'Where did you hear this?'

'Oh Samson, your name is legend. Your deeds precede you. What I would like to know though is how? How do you find the strength?'

Samson became uneasy, his dream coming back to him unprompted. The idea of the Philistine King wishing to kill him and knowing the source of his strength was key.

'It is fine. You have no need to tell me. I am simply curious how one man kills so many Philistine soldiers at his bride's feast without so much as a sword. They say the power is from Yahweh. I am not convinced.' Delilah's words would have been innocent to the Nazarite if not for all that had transpired recently.

'My strength is a gift from Yahweh but the secret to it remains mine and mine alone. That is the pledge of a Nazarite.'

Delilah shrugged as though the answer meant nothing to her, but Samson could see she was annoyed.

'Are you sure you will not accompany us?' She ventured one last time.

'I am sure.'

Delilah reached up and patted his cheek again, right where she had left her kiss and smiled in a way that made Samson's blood run hot. Without another word she spun round, her braid almost hitting him in the face and skipped from the cook-house, Aggie trailing devotedly behind.

As soon as they were out of earshot, Aggie leant in close. 'What was that all about?'

'I have a plan Aggie. It won't bring Ebony back, but it will save my family.'

'Delilah, Samson is not a toy to be trifled with. He is a Nazarite, a man of God.' Aggie had a sinking feeling that her meddling may very well have set in motion a different path, one that may well serve Dagon after all.

# Chapter 23

Delilah left Aggie picking through a fruit stall and made her way to the temple of Dagon. Majdi was exactly where she expected to find him, waiting near the entrance, hovering over anyone who entered, hoping to pry coin or favour from their hands.

The blood drained from the Priest's face as Delilah approached. 'Majdi, so lovely to see you again.'

Delilah took great joy in seeing the man squirm. She knew he had seen her throw Dagon's soldiers around the courtyard. She still did not understand how she had managed it, but during the attack, she had seen a glimpse of something or nothing. Exactly what, she was unsure, but Aggie knew more than she was sharing and Delilah had a fairly good idea how to draw the truth out.

'I, I.' The Priest swallowed and fidgeted uncomfortably. 'Delilah. None of this was my idea.'

'I know Majdi. Kaamill is behind this. Tell him I will get what he desires but if anything happens to either of my parents, I will come for all of you. Starting with you Majdi.'

'There is no need for threats.'

'Really! No need you say. Where is Ebony? Is she still alive? Am I too late? Did you sacrifice her to Dagon already?' Delilah's voice gradually rose until everyone in the temple could clearly hear her words.

A tall dark woman with large hooped earrings and vivid makeup scurried from the temple, followed by two eunuchs, eyes downcast and hands clasped across their chest.

'Please keep your voice down.' Majdi begged, taking Delilah carefully by the arm and leading her aside.

'Why? Everyone knows you sacrifice virgins upon Dagon's altar.' Delilah smiled as more wealthy patrons vacated the temple, embarrassingly hiding their faces in the hopes of remaining anonymous.

The voice was a hiss and if Delilah had thought she made Majdi look pale, whoever stood behind her now had him shrinking into the crevices of the stone walls.

'Delilah. We meet again.' The young woman slowly turned to find herself surrounded by dark wings that flickered from black to transparent and back again.

She frowned at the phenomenon and calmly followed the torso of the figure before her up, until she met his eyes. They blazed like a furnace and for a moment, Delilah grew transfixed. 'I hear you agreed to our arrangement.' The dark angel's voice echoed in her chest.

'Where is Kaamill?' Delilah locked her gaze with Dagon and refused to flinch.

'Kaamill is no longer required my dear, now that we have finally met in the flesh.' Dagon stroked Delilah's cheek and a ripple of desire flooded the girl. Visions of Ebony quickly forced the emotion aside and Dagon physically flinched at the action.

'You are strong. I knew you would be Delilah. I never choose the weak ones, like your friend Ebony, is it? She would never have been my queen.'

Delilah laughed, the sound a mixture of mockery and flirtatiousness. 'Your queen. You threaten me. You take my only friend away from me and now you propose to me. You are beyond evil Dagon.'

'Now is that Asherah speaking or really you Delilah?'

'Asherah?'

Dagon shrugged away his lapse. 'You have work to do Delilah. Come and see me when you know the Nazarite's secret.'

'Delilah, where in Heaven's name are you?' Aggie called across the square, the sound filtering through the temple doorway. Dagon disappeared and Delilah looked around to find Majdi nowhere in sight.

Delilah wrapped her shawl around her shoulders and left the temple as Aggie approached the steps guardedly.

'You and I need to talk.' The woman waved a finger at the girl accusingly.

'Yes, we do. No more secrets Asherah. That is who you are, is it not?'

Asherah frowned, screwed up her face and took a moment to consider the girl. 'I do not usually reveal myself to humans, only my Priestesses and that you are not child.'

'No, but I am a quick learner.'

'I can see that. When did you realise?'

'Just now, when Dagon sensed your presence and thought you had, how shall I put it, invaded my body again.'

'Oh stop with the melodramatics. If I had not done so before, you would have been dead.'

'That is not entirely true. Dagon wants me to do something. He had no intention of killing me.'

Asherah shook her head. 'Too smart for your own good. Let us get back to the estate and we can talk at length. When you asked me to help get you out of the estate to the market, I should have known you were up to something.'

Delilah smiled and took the goddess's arm in hers. 'Shall we go then?'

****

The tavern was dark and the smell of stale ale drifted into Samson's nostrils as he opened the rough-sawn wooden door.

'What are we doing here?' Aviv ducked below the low doorway and followed his friend onto the sawdust covered floor.

'I need to find someone.'

Aviv sighed with frustration. 'I wish you would tell me what is going on? First Delilah suddenly goes from being unconscious to heading off to the market of all places and now you drag me into this hovel to find *someone*.'

'Let us just say I have a bad feeling. The Philistine king is planning to take control of the Israelites and he has to go through me to do so.'

Aviv nodded and raised two fingers to the barman as Samson tossed a copper coin on the bar and two mugs of ale, the foam spilling to the bench, were slammed down in front of both men.

'Yes, but you have your god on your side. You are too strong to die at any Philistine's hands. A whole army could not kill you, they know that.'

'Exactly my point. So in order to kill me they need to know what gives me that strength, right?'

Aviv suddenly began to see where his friend was going.

'And no one knows that, not even you my friend.' Samson took a quick swig of his ale.

'So, that is easy, make sure you do not tell anyone and all will be well.'

'That is where the bad feeling is coming from Aviv. I have a suspicion that keeping my secret is going to become difficult.'

Aviv lifted the mug to his lips and savoured the ale. 'Hovel or no, this ale is quite spectacular.'

'Ah, there is the man I am here to see. Stay here, I will be back in a moment. Try not to get into any trouble.' Samson leant on his friend's shoulder as he rose to leave.

Aviv scanned the room. Other than the barman and Samson's *someone*, there was only one very drunk shepherd slumped with his head on the table by the dormant fireplace and a young woman cleaning tables near the small shuttered window by the door.

A smile crept across the merchant's face as the woman lifted her face and her eyes smiled in his direction.

Chapter 24

'She has created her own path, one I am not sure is ordained? Has father shared anything, with anyone?' Asherah begged her sisters.

Anath shook her head, her long golden hair spilling freely in the weightlessness of the Veil between humanity and the eternal realm.

'You should speak with Michael. This could change everything, the prophecy, the future. Everything!' Astarte waved her hands erratically until Asherah took both of them in hers and hushed her sister.

'How about you find out what you can from Moloch?' Asherah spoke, still holding Astarte's hands.

'He no longer trusts me. Lilith has his ear now.' Astarte looked truly crestfallen, small tears sprang from her eyes, evaporating into sparkling dust.

'He is not for you Astarte, you know this now. He has wandered from the way.'

'But he is still good deep down inside, I know it Asherah. He just does not embrace change. We had

Father to ourselves for so long before humanity came to exist.'

'You sympathise with him.' Asherah patted her sister's sweet face. 'I understand. You should step away from this fight Astarte, your heart is elsewhere.'

'No, the prophecy, the Prince of Peace. It must come to pass.'

'You girls should not assume the Veil hides you from others.'

All three goddesses spun around, their hair trailing after them like ribbons on the wind.

'Michael, we did not hear you approach.'

The Archangel smiled at the obvious statement. The goddesses giggled like small girls, found out while stealing sweets from the forbidden stores.

'I am so glad you are here.' Asherah floated toward the angel who stood nearly twice her height. 'Delilah strays from the prophecy.'

'The path is written Asherah. We have had this discussion on many an occasion. You really do not need to meddle but I know you must.'

'You do not understand Michael. Delilah plans to deceive Samson, then deceive Dagon.' Asherah struggled to keep the panic from her voice.

Michael embraced her in his soft wings for a moment until she relaxed once more.

'That is much better.' Michael spoke with genuine care. 'Now, what do you know of the Prophecy?' Michael coaxed patiently.

'I know the temple must fall. I know that Delilah and Samson must join forces to bring this about.'

'Yes, that is true. But you do not know how this is to come to pass, is that correct?

'I do not.'

'Then trust that the path is set, the outcome will not change. It is what happens after the temple falls that will truly set the course for the future.'

'I do not understand.' Asherah frowned and stepped back to study Michael's face.

'What do you mean Michael?' Anath moved closer to hear while Astarte waited behind her warrior sister.

'You will see Asherah. We all have our part to play. As you said, you were born to meddle and meddle you will. You will know when the time is right. Trust the Father, trust me.'

Michael opened his wings but no sound was emitted, he simply vanished beyond the Veil leaving the three goddesses staring at each other, mouths open and brows furrowed in confusion.

'I really hate it when he does that.' Astarte grumbled.

'What? Disappears?' Anath folded her arms across her chest. 'Me too.'

'No, when he answers a question with even more questions.' Astarte sighed in frustration.

Chapter 25

'You go on ahead. I need to check with the staff on a few housekeeping matters. I will meet you in the courtyard shortly.' Aviv directed Samson on as he turned to move down an adjoining corridor.

'Bring wine.'

'Of course. You know you never have to ask.' Aviv waved his hand over his shoulder dismissively and Samson smiled to himself.

The sunlight was filtering into the long walkway as the Nazarite made his way to the courtyard, the smell of flowers wafting on the warm breeze.

'Samson, I was wondering if you could help me?' Delilah almost pounced on the man as soon as he set foot on the coarse gravel of the courtyard.

Samson stopped and smiled as he took in the beauty of the young woman before him. Her hair was tied back in a tight braid. She wore a short tunic and her bronze legs had a sheen about them that threatened to send shivers down the man's spine.

'Of course Delilah. What do you need?'

The young woman pulled out a long dagger and Samson took a reflexive step backwards. 'I need you to teach me how to use this.' Delilah smiled mischievously and stepped forward, waving her weapon recklessly.

'Why?' Samson looked to see if Aviv was anywhere near.

'Just because. Why do you have to question everything?' Delilah placed her hands on her hips, nearly stabbing the dagger into herself in the process.

'Be careful with that. Where did you get a dagger anyway?' Samson stepped forward and took the weapon from her easily. Holding it aloft while the girl protested.

'Give it back.' Delilah jumped for the blade but she barely reached Samson's armpit. There was no way she had any hope of retrieving the dagger.

'I will when you tell me why.' Samson insisted. 'By all accounts you fought like a lion when the Priests came for Ebony. Why do you need to learn the blade?'

Aviv walked into the courtyard in that moment, Delilah's hand grabbing at Samson's with her skirt rising high enough to expose the young woman's upper thigh and buttocks. Samson saw his friend's face and laughed aloud as Aviv juggled the tray of drinks and quickly regained his composure.

'But first, you need to lower you arm.' Delilah almost growled and Samson lifted both his hands into the air in submission. 'Really, I am not trying to boss you around.' He nodded his head behind Delilah and she swung around to see Aviv's smile spreading across his face.

'For the goddesses' sake Aviv, stop gawking. It is nothing you have not seen before.'

'Since when have you followed the goddess?' Aviv chose not to discuss what he had or had not seen, especially of Delilah's person. That was likely to open a lion's den he had no intentions of walking into.

Delilah shrugged as Aggie joined the group. 'I cannot say for sure. Maybe as recently as today.' Delilah smiled at Aggie who muttered under her breath and Samson looked from the old woman to the girl with confusion.

'Aviv, convince Samson that it is time to teach me to fight.'

'I am not getting involved in this, sorry.' Aviv placed the wine on the table bowed out of the courtyard wisely without turning his back on Delilah who responded by collecting up a cushion from the

divan and throwing it at the man, hitting him full in
the head.

Samson was still laughing when Delilah looked
back at the Nazarite. 'Why on earth are you not
willing to help me?'

'I never said I would not help you Delilah. I
simply asked why?'

Frustrated, the girl threw the dagger on the
ground, narrowly missing Samson's foot and stormed
out of the courtyard with balled fists and her braid
swinging furiously.

Samson looked at Aggie and the old woman
shrugged her shoulders, placed a tray of dried fruit
and flat bread she was carrying down on the table
before the divan and moved to follow her charge.

'Do you know why she wants me to train her?'
Samson gently took the woman's arm as she turned to
leave. The tingling was gone before it began, but the
Nazarite had felt it. A flash of his dream leapt into his
mind and he dropped Aggie's hand with a gasp.

'All will be revealed when she is ready, of that I
am sure.' Aggie patted the Nazarite on the shoulder
and left him without another word.

Samson slumped down in the divan, collecting
a handful of dried fruit and a mug of cool wine on the
way. He threw the handful in his mouth and rubbed

his chin with his thumb and forefinger as he chewed. Finally, he gave up his contemplation and sat back to enjoy what was left of the afternoon sun.

****

Delilah watched the guards walk around the estate. They had been doubled, if not tripled since Ebony had been taken.

Samson had forbidden Delilah from leaving the estate unescorted ever since her trip with Aggie to the market. Luckily, he had no idea she had visited Dagon's temple or he would have been furious.

The young woman felt torn. Maybe if she had never been to the temple, never been confronted by the god of the Philistines she might have been able to just play along with Samson and Aviv until she found herself a wealthy husband, but now everything had changed.

Now Dagon would kill her family if she did not tell them Samson's secret. She had grown fond of him. He had not ratted her out to her parents, instead he had offered to act as her benefactor.

She knew he had an ulterior motive. She could see the thoughts running through his mind when he looked at her. The man might be a Judge of the Israelites, a Zealot for their god but he was as easily read as the pictures on the temple wall.

Aggie mounted the steps to the battlements that surrounded the estate walls with melodramatic moans and groans.

'You can cut the act now Asherah.' Delilah sat with her head on her hands and her elbows on her knees. Her short dress covered nothing and the goddess cleared her throat and frowned at the girl's lack of modesty.

'No one can see from all the way up here and what do you care? You are the goddess of fertility. In the lands of our ancestors, your worshippers were whores.'

'That is not technically true at all. My Priestesses serve me in whatever way they see fit. There are very few vocations available to a single woman; you of all people should know that!'

Asherah sat down easily next to the girl and crossed her legs under her peasant dress.

'Why are you here Asherah?' Delilah pulled her legs closer and turned to face the goddess.

'It is too long a story to share with one as young as you my dear.'

'Humour me.' Delilah's face left no room for discussion.

'Look, I am not at liberty to tell you everything, in fact the Creator would likely punish me severely if

I were to explain it all but in short, I am here to protect you from Dagon.'

'And who exactly is Dagon to you?'

'That comes under the "I am not at liberty to discuss" category.'

'How did you know I would need help and protection from Dagon and why me, why not Ebony? Why not all the other women who have died on his sacrificial altar?' Delilah was trying desperately to control her anger.

'I am not even supposed to be here Delilah let alone explain all the nuances of the eternal realm.'

'Why are you here then?'

'Because I like to meddle alright. Just thank your lucky stars I do.'

'I am not in any danger Asherah, not right now anyway. Dagon wants me for himself, at least that is what he has told me. It is Samson who is in danger.'

'Samson is a Nazarite. He signed up to die for the Creator many years ago. He would have died a hundred times already if not for his divine strength. Samson will be just fine child. Do not let Dagon manipulate you like this.'

'He has threatened my family Asherah. He has told me he will kill them if I do not discover Samson's secret. You are a goddess, you can keep my family and Samson safe.'

'Technically I cannot.'

'*Technically*, since when do goddesses have technicalities to deal with?'

'Since the beginning of time Delilah.'

'What am I to do?' A tear rolled down the distraught woman's face and she took a deep breath to try and compose herself.

'Tell the truth child. The truth will set you free. The truth is the only way to resolve any issue.'

'Even when it hurts?'

'Especially when it hurts.' Asherah wrapped her arm around Delilah. The tingling sensation passed quickly and Delilah relaxed onto the goddess's shoulder, her breathing growing instantly slow and deep.

Samson took the long way to his room. As he passed the battlements he eyed Aggie with her arm wrapped protectively around Delilah. He waved up as he made his rounds, ensuring each guard was alert and ready in case the temple Priests returned to try and capture Delilah.

Aggie waved back nonchalantly and patted Delilah's shoulder. 'I wish you could all be Angel's

child, then this fight would be over before it had
begun.' Delilah stirred but did not wake.

Chapter 26

Aviv fought his way through the crowd that seemed to part with ease for Samson who followed behind. They made their way to their allocated seats, the smell of stale sweat and ale filling the brightly lit building.

Samson had seen the gold coin Aviv slipped the doorman in exchange for the prime position and nodded his appreciation as they took their place.

'How much did you say you bet on him? Samson leant in close to speak so no one nearby would hear.

'Ten gold pieces.' Aviv smiled confidently.

'That is madness. He is half the man's size. He will be flat on the ground in the first round.' Samson puffed his chest out with authority. He knew fighting men and Aviv's fighter was half a head shorter and at least a third lighter than his opponent.

'Just sit back and wait. You will see.' Aviv put his hands together behind his head and leaned back in his chair knowingly as a scantily clad serving girl placed his ale down on the table, showing him her ample cleavage with obvious intent.

The arena was like nothing Samson had seen before. There was a sawdust circle in the centre surrounded by a row of benches. The whole area slowly rose from the middle with more seats and small tables attached to the back of each set, allowing patrons to drink and relax as they watched each bout.

Yet there was no one sitting for this match. Nearly everyone was on their feet almost as soon as the fight had begun. The smaller competitor moved with lightning speed, upending his opponent onto the ground in a blur. He landed heavily into the man's chest, knocking the wind out of him as a loud crack reverberated around the audience.

Moans and jeers could be heard from every direction as men threw down their betting slips in disgust.

'How did you know?' Samson's mouth was hanging open, his eyes wide with astonishment.

'I just know these things.' Aviv winked mischievously and Samson frowned his mistrust.

The two combatants made their way to their changing rooms, the larger on a stretcher while four dancing girls took to the sawdust. The crowd that had begun to leave stopped and returned to their seats to the sound of jingling belly dancers and beating drums.

'I think I might be on my way my friend. I have a few people to visit to see if anyone has more information about what the King is up to.'

'Wait a minute Samson. I will join you. Just let me offer my condolences to the losing party.'

Aviv jumped from his seat, made his way to the end aisle and took the steps two at a time, down until he reached the arena below. Samson stood to follow him but his friend did not go all the way down the long tunnel to the fighter's rooms. Instead, he handed coins to the doorman and patted him on the back.

Samson waited for his friend to return. He shook his head at his own stupidity. Aviv really was not the man he had thought he was and a sudden sense of unease started in the pit of the big man's stomach.

'All good now. Let us head off. Where to?' Aviv smiled as he made his way out of the compact stadium.

'You paid the bigger fighter to take the fall.' It was not a question and Aviv turned to face Samson, his finger on his lips.

'Shhh! You trying to get me killed?'

'You cheated!'

'Come on outside and we can talk about this. I know you are not fond of alternative methods.'

They were finally outside and Aviv moved as far away from the arena as quickly as he could.

'That is an understatement and you know it. You remember what happened last time I witnessed cheating?'

'Yes, yes of course I do but that was when someone cheated you. I have not cheated you my friend, only those men in there willingly giving their coin in a wager. There is no harm in it.' Aviv tried to reassure Samson.

'I killed thirty men and paid my debt to my wife's family with the dead men's uniforms.' Samson continued as though Aviv had not spoken a word.

'Samson, that was hardly fair retribution. The men who cheated you got away with it and you killed thirty innocent men. The Philistines still remember the incident with great disdain.'

Samson clenched his fist and Aviv ducked under the blow he knew was coming. 'Come on Samson, you have had too much to drink. I will take you home.'

'I am not drunk Aviv. I am angry.'

'Why, because I did a few men out of a few coins? The fighter is happy. His manager is happy. Everyone got paid. What is the issue?'

'Cheating is just not right.' Samson's anger was abating and he looked like sadness was overtaking him. 'They killed my wife Aviv. First, they took her from me, then they gave her to another man and then they burned her alive with her father because I killed those Philistines.'

Aviv watched Samson's shoulders sink low and moved in to console his friend. He had seen this melancholy take over the big man only a few times before and it never ended well, not for Samson, not for anyone within fighting distance of him.

'I know Samson. I am sorry my deeds brought back your nightmares. Let us forget about your informants and head straight to the estate.'

Samson shook his head. 'No, we must see if they have learnt anything.' Aviv shrugged and moved off as Samson did, seemingly recovered.

They walked down one alley and then another and onto the open market square. It was dark and empty with little light but the moon and Aviv felt more than a little apprehensive.

A woman in a dark hooded cape darted into the temple and Aviv paid no attention until Samson stopped in his tracks.

'That looked like Delilah.'

'How can you possibly tell in this poor light?' Aviv whispered, his anxiety growing. 'She would never leave the estate, especially not to go to the temple after what happened to her friend, surely?'

'We need to get closer.' Samson ducked into the shadow of a nearby awning. By day it would usually be out and covering the fruit stand of the owner that resided there but at night, it was tucked away and tied up to prevent the wind from blowing it away in a storm. Both men held to the thin shadow that existed below it.

'Samson. Why on earth would Delilah go to the temple of Dagon and without Aggie?'

'That my friend is what I am trying to discover.' Samson whispered and pointed to the next shadow. Both men scurried like thieves until they were once more hidden in the darkness and waited.

****

Delilah knew she had to give Dagon something, anything that would keep her parents safe. Asherah could not or would not do anything and she had no intention of asking Samson, let alone giving up his secret to an evil god like Dagon.

It was late and Delilah was not sure anyone would even be at the temple but something told her that if she called Dagon, he would come. Her heart was in her throat and her palms were moist with sweat as she slipped into the entrance and made her way to the carved wall where Dagon had last appeared.

She took a deep breath and almost choked as a sound came from behind her. She swung around to find the Priest, with his bald head and hawk-like eyes staring at her by the faint candlelight of the altar.

'Delilah. So nice of you to return so quickly. Dagon wishes to know what you have discovered.'

'I think you can bind him. With fresh bow strings. I heard him talking to his friend about it.'

'You look nervous child.' The Priest moved closer and Delilah forced herself not to shiver. 'Come now. I have something that will soothe your anxiety.' The Priest reached out to touch the young woman but stopped as goose bumps spread out around his body.

A low growl sounded from the temple, as though the walls were going to close in at any moment and the Priest moved away from Delilah in an unrecognisable blur.

'It seems the Lord Dagon wishes to thank you for your information. Now run along child. Leave everything to us.'

'What about my parents?' Delilah suddenly felt bold. Her family was all she had, even though they were so far away. Thoughts of them threatened to bring tears to her eyes, but the young woman took a deep breath and puffed her chest out.

'Your family will be fine if you tell the truth and we succeed. If not...' The Priest shrugged and left the rest of his answer unsaid.

Delilah heard a noise outside and turned to look. By the time she looked back, the Priest was gone and the candles by the altar were beginning to snuff out. The girl physically trembled and shuddered for a moment before lifting her hooded robe and scurrying for the exit.

She ran carefully through the streets, avoiding the darkest alleyways as much as possible. As she neared the estate she stopped to risk a view behind her. She could not exactly explain it, but the hairs on the back of her neck told her someone was watching her.

Seeing nothing, she opened the small door alongside the large ornate estate gates and sneaked through, checking over her shoulder one last time before locking the door.

Chapter 27

Samson had spent the night tossing and turning. The memory of his wife's death, the loss of so many men at his hands weighed heavily on his heart. Then there was Delilah. She drove him to distraction. He would do anything to keep her safe, but she did not value her safety as he did.

He rose from bed and splashed his face with fresh cool water. As he peered into the brass mirror at his long hair, tied back into seven braids he could not help but wonder if his vow was worth the sacrifice.

A Nazarite, a man of the Israelite God had him bound to the will of Yahweh in everything he did but it was his own temper that killed all those Philistines. It was his own lack of control that gave them cause to burn his wife alive.

He would do anything to ensure that Delilah did not share such a fate. Samson took a soft cloth and wiped his face before dressing in his tunic and tying his leather armour and weapons in place.

As he left his room a sense of purpose filled his spirit. He strode through the halls of Aviv's estate and shook his head at the ornate carvings, expensive cushions and furniture he passed. Finally, he made his way to the training yard to join Aviv and his guards.

The sun was barely rising in the sky and the soft grey hue of predawn filled Samson with wonder at the perfection of creation. The morning was a beautiful time of the day. The newness of it, the freshness, the chance to start over filled his heart and lifted his guilt.

The serenity was broken as the Nazarite drew closer to the fighting men. Aviv had his arm around Delilah's waist and was almost caressing her as he showed her how to hold her dagger. Samson could not quite explain the feeling that welled in the pit of his stomach but he knew he needed to release it before it exploded all on its own.

Aviv must have seen or sensed his friend's approach because he released Delilah quickly, but smoothly and spun her gently around to see Samson's arrival.

'What is she doing here?' The words had left his lips before he could stop them.

'Training. What does it look like I am doing? At least Aviv understands.' Delilah tried to swallow her fury. 'I thought of all people you would, but…' she finally stopped ranting before she lost her composure and turned back to Aviv, hoisted her dagger and nodded for him to continue.

Samson sighed and gained control of his emotions. He approached his friend and Delilah and took the weapon from her hands as easily as he did before.

'You need to understand Delilah.'

'Leave me alone Samson. You obviously do not care if Dagon's Priests come for me untrained and unequipped.' Delilah's frustration was all over her face and Samson stepped forward, threw the dagger aside and took both the young woman's wrists gently in his hands.

'I care more than I should, but you need to understand Delilah, you cannot fight like a man, you must learn to fight like a woman.'

The words could have been offensive, but Samson's eyes had softened and his grip was calm, almost soothing. Delilah stopped struggling against him and relaxed. The Nazarite released her with obvious regret.

'You are playing a dangerous game. I will do what I can to help you protect yourself but please be careful Delilah.'

She took a deep, slow breath. Maybe she had misunderstood Samson. Could he genuinely care for her, not just want her as a possession? She shook the thought away. Caring was dangerous.

A sudden surge of confidence filled her heart and Delilah stepped forward, touching Samson's cheek with her soft hand. Samson gasped as a tingle exploded with her touch.

He took her hand in his and held it, close to his lips as though about to kiss it. Aviv cleared his throat and turned to his guards who had stopped their practice to observe the commotion.

'What are you all gawking at? Get back to training.' Aviv looked back over his shoulder at Samson and Delilah and grinned mischievously.

'Show the girl how to fight like a woman then man. What are you waiting for?' Aviv winked over Delilah's shoulder.

Samson let Delilah's hand drop away reluctantly. 'I have no idea how you managed to man-handle the temple's soldiers when they attacked but the men said you were fierce like a lion.'

Delilah shrugged. She could hardly tell the man she was possessed by a goddess at the time. 'I think fear took control.'

'Hmm. Some people do gain amazing strength when they are frightened. But you cannot always rely on this, in fact it can be dangerous. The temple soldiers are more likely to use stealth next time. They know we are prepared to protect you.'

Delilah smiled. It was unlikely Dagon would send soldiers again. He took Ebony to threaten her. Other than Samson, there was no one else here to hold over her. 'How do I protect myself from such an attack?'

Samson moved in closely and reached over Delilah's shoulder from behind. Her skin tingled at the touch of his chest on her back and for a moment she thought he might kiss her but instead he held her tightly with his arm around her neck.

'That is hardly comfortable.' She protested, gripping his strong bronzed forearm away from her throat so she could speak.

'This is the most likely attack. A coward comes from behind, he wraps his arm around your neck and if he is taller, he lifts you from your feet, choking you into unconsciousness or worse.'

'Such an encouraging picture you paint. How do I get out of this then?' Delilah touched Samson's arm more firmly and the hairs rose at the warmth of her fingers but he quickly returned his attention to training and squeezed gently.

'Now, I will not use the same force for now. I want to show you what to do first. How do you think you could get away?'

Delilah pinched Samson, she tried to bite him, she kicked him with her legs but nothing stopped the big man holding her helplessly.

'You are not filling me with confidence Samson. What do I do?' Frustration began to take its toll and Delilah grumbled despite trying hard not to be ungrateful.

'Losing your temper will not help you escape. Here, try this. See the space near my elbow?' Delilah nodded as she looked out the corner of her eye.

'Turn your head to face the space. Yes, perfect, now you can breathe. If I were holding you tightly, you would have become unconscious by now.'

'What good is that? You still have me by the neck.'

'True. We will learn this in stages. Once you know all the steps, you can practise them together, getting quicker and quicker until you do them so fast, your attacker has no chance to hold you.

Delilah was growing more confident. 'Alright, what next?'

'Next you elbow me in the ribs, you drop to the ground so I have to suddenly take all your weight and then you grab my thumb and twist it away like this. If this is done successively and quickly, you will get the space you need to escape.'

Samson was just about to run through the moves again when Delilah counter attacked. She did exactly what he had told her to do and if it had been any other man, it would have worked. Samson chose to let her win this one. Confidence was important he knew.

'Whoohoo!' Delilah cried out excitedly and Aviv's guards joined in with a cheer.

'Well done but do not get too excited just yet.' Samson moved forward for a frontal choke-hold and the lesson continued.

# Chapter 28

'Will you take me with you when you go out tonight?' Delilah stood with Samson in the courtyard, their afternoon training now complete.

Samson wiped his glistening torso with a cloth, while Delilah felt suddenly dirty and unattractive with her sweat-stained tunic and flushed cheeks.

'Where we are going is no place for a young woman.'

'So you are visiting with whores.' Delilah spoke without any malice. Men had needs and she understood that Samson was just like any other man in so many ways.

'No. No. Of course not but it is hardly a place where women frequent. There are, how should I put it…?' Samson wiped his fingers through his hair and tossed the cloth aside nervously. 'The establishment is full of barely dressed women and men who have rather unrefined manners.'

'You forget where you found me Samson. I am not unaccustomed to unruly men. I could tell you some stories.' Delilah smiled wickedly.

Samson held up his hand feigning disinterest. 'Please, I would rather you did not.'

'Oh Samson.' Delilah wrapped her arms around the man's waist, her face buried into his chest. 'You like to think of me as an innocent little girl. How charming.'

'No.' Samson felt the heat from Delilah's body. Her scent was intoxicating and he fought for control. 'That is not it. It is more the thought of what I would do to anyone who did not treat you as the fine woman you are.'

Delilah was surprised once more by the tenderness of the warrior. 'I am sorry for teasing you.' She smiled a genuinely shy smile. 'I would like to join you though. I have been cooped up in here for days and I am so, so bored.'

Samson shook his head, trying to figure out how he could say no. Keeping her close was a good idea. She could not sneak off to the temple if she were with him, but the tavern they planned on attending was no place for her.'

'You can come, but the moment things get rowdy, I am taking you home, you understand?'

'Yes sir!' Delilah saluted, much like the guards did when they saw him or Aviv in the courtyard.

****

Asherah floated above the courtyard as she watched Samson and Delilah training and talking together. She fought the urge to interfere with their relationship but it was difficult.

'What are you doing sister?' Moloch smiled as he flipped a gold coin in his palm.

'I am observing my charge Moloch and please, I have asked you before, do not call me that.' The goddess fought the urge to put her hands on her hips. She knew Moloch was goading her.

'But you are my sister, as Dagon is your brother.' Moloch's features softened and he swept the long lock of loose hair over his ear, exposing his dark eyes.

'We are related, yes, but brothers and sisters do not wage war against each other. They do not seek to kill one another.'

'I have no intention of ending your existence Asherah or any other of my brethren and it is you who wage war against us. We just see things a little differently. Why are you all so intolerant of our feelings?'

Delilah watched her brother closely. Was he being genuine? Was he teasing her or trying to distract her? It was so hard to trust him after all that had transpired.

'Oh Moloch. The humans have free-will because they live down there.' Asherah pointed to the ground below her. 'We on the other hand are not offered it because Heaven is not a democracy. We are not equal to the Creator, we are his creations.'

'But we have evolved just as they have.' Moloch nodded at Samson and Delilah. 'They began many years ago as little more than animals and now they have a society with laws and kings, art and music, craftsmen and farmers.'

'You sound like you admire them Moloch. I always assumed you hated them.' Asherah raised an eyebrow in question. Where was this coming from?

'I never said I hated them. I just have no wish to share our home with them and eternity is not for them, it is for us.'

'That is not our choice to make. They were to have eternal life in the beginning.'

'Yes, until they got too smart for their own good.'

'Yes and then Dagon and those like him taught them even more of what they were never meant to know. The Fallen taught them magic, bred with them to create a whole new race. So many mistakes.' Asherah shook her head and sighed, suddenly feeling tired.

'Exactly, Asherah and the Creator knew of them all. Why did he not stop the Nephilim from coming to be? Why did he not stop Dagon and our brethren before they waivered? It is all a great game and you are just playing along for Father's enjoyment.' Moloch kept his distance, but Asherah could sense his agitation.

'I refuse to believe that Moloch. Please, just go away and leave me alone.'

'I thought I was the one to run away from a losing debate.' Moloch smiled cheekily and Asherah began to understand Astarte's weakness for him. Before she could answer, Moloch disappeared from the earthly realm and Asherah was left with more questions.

****

The tavern was an eye-opener for Delilah. Sure, she had stolen coin and done favours for the Priest of the temple before and then there was her experience with Ebony and her friend which had certainly expanded her education, but what Samson called entertainment was an entirely new experience.

From the moment she entered, she had deflected hands that came from nowhere and disappeared just as quickly.

181

Aviv, Samson and Delilah took a seat in a dark corner just as a heavy woman with large breasts and too much eye make-up almost threw mugs of ale onto the table before them.

She smiled a toothless grin at the men and both fought the urge to cringe.

'That be all? If you want anything else, just give me a holla now. I do mean anything else.' The buxom lady winked and Samson and Aviv were well mannered enough to smile in reply.

'She would eat you alive man.' Samson whispered into Aviv's ear as the woman swayed her ample hips and gave another toothless grin focussed on the smaller of the two men.

'I have no doubt, none at all my friend.' Both men lifted their drinks and Delilah sniffed hers sceptically.

'You have never drunk ale?' Aviv raised an eyebrow.

'Never. Wine, spirts, some of the finest but never ale.'

'Well then, your first new experience.'

'Not my first,' Delilah grinned at Aviv's surprise, 'but definitely a new experience.

'Your family served the Philistine King?' Samson asked, understanding why ale would not have reached the girl's table.

'We did. For as long as I could remember until father disagreed with the King and we were exiled.'

'Well you are back in the lap of luxury and soon we will have what we came for and you can return to your family, with a suitable husband to make your father happy.' Aviv knew he was teasing and did his best to see if Samson would rise to the bait. He had watched Samson with Delilah. He knew how his friend felt, even if he was unwilling or unable to share his feelings.

'I am not sure I want to return, or want to take a husband.' Delilah sipped her ale nonchalantly and grimaced at the flavour.

Samson was not sure if he was offended or relieved but he managed to hide feelings, at least from Aviv. 'I miss my family, more than I thought I would to be honest, but I have enjoyed the freedom here. My parents were always worried and even though Samson does a great job of making up where they left off, I still have so much more time to myself.'

Delilah saw something out the corner of her eye as she finished speaking. Samson and Aviv took another swig of their drinks and failed to notice her fleeting distraction

For a moment, she thought she had been seeing things but then she saw him again. Kaamill! *What was he doing here?*

'I am here to see you my dear.' Kaamill spoke into her mind and Delilah struggled to keep her features even. She had no idea how to respond, but she was not leaving Samson's side anytime soon so he was going to be out of luck.

Kaamill disappeared from sight and Delilah released the breath she had been holding.

'Are you alright?' Samson touched her arm and she smiled. She almost snuggled into his protective arm, but resisted the urge. 'You look pale. Maybe we should take you home.'

'No, I am fine Samson. The night is young.' The sound of drums made Delilah jump and Aviv and Samson laughed aloud at her shock.

'The entertainment begins.' Aviv leant back in his seat. The wooden bench he chose had a high back and was built into the corner. It was scattered with soft cushions that threatened to take over the space with their bulk.

As the drumming grew louder, a small troupe of dancers entered the room. They walked between the tables and spun their veils around in the air as they danced. Two men, their skin almost black and their chests exposed spun tiny pots on chains with fire alight within.

Delilah almost giggled like a child as the group of dancers made their way to the stage at the front of the tavern. The room had begun to fill with pipe smoke and a large ornate pipe appeared before Delilah on the table.

'I thought you were a holy man. What kind of holy man drinks ale, consorts with *dancers* and partakes of opium?'

'My oath is my own Delilah and I never promised to refrain from the pleasures of life to serve.'

'Nice to know.' Delilah smiled as she watched Aviv take a deep inhalation of the shared pipe. As the night drew on, Samson grew more relaxed than Delilah had ever seen him.

The hair on the back of her neck stood up as the toothless woman returned. Her eyes glinted and realisation struck Delilah before the words entered her head. *Tonight we put your information to the test. Let us hope you are right and you have not lied to me.'*

Delilah watched as the serving woman put another ale in front of Samson and dropped something into it. Her mind raced. She never expected to be witness to Dagon's attempt to kidnap Samson.

She struggled with her choice. Say nothing and put Samson's life at risk or tell him the woman had drugged him and that the woman was in reality, Dagon the dark god. How could she explain such a thing? He would never believe her.

'Oh Asherah. What have I done?' Delilah allowed the words to form in her mind before she realised it.

Chapter 29

Samson and Aviv made their way out of the tavern with Delilah close behind. 'I did not drink that much Aviv.'

'Sure, big man. Keep telling yourself that. Just because you are strong, does not mean opium and ale cannot take you down like the rest of us.' Aviv laughed aloud.

The trio took a turn down an alley and Aviv stopped in front of Delilah, his posture alert, making her instantly nervous. She had been expecting an attack, but that did not mean she was prepared for it.

'Step aside merchant. We have no quarrel with you. Take the girl and leave the Israelite.'

'As invincible as he is, I am not inclined to help you give him a headache friends. Why not move on and save us all a long night' Aviv took Delilah's arm and gently drew her behind him. He looked over his shoulder at Samson who seemed quite oblivious to the commotion.

'Have it your way.' The leader moved forward in the darkness. It was impossible to see he was a soldier of Dagon until he was almost upon them. Aviv drew his dagger and pushed Delilah aside. Samson seemed to get even more unsteady on his feet and Aviv frowned in confusion.

'No one harm the girl.' The soldier called to everyone behind him.

'Great, give the girl a pass. What about the merchant?' Aviv flipped his dagger.

The attack was swift and unprovoked. Delilah tried to join the fight to support Samson until one of the soldiers grabbed her from behind. 'Now, now. You know you just need to stand by and you will be fine,' he whispered in her ear. His hot foul-smelling breath made her shudder.

Delilah heard Samson's voice step by step in her mind as she moved her head so she could breathe, jabbed the man in the ribs with her elbow, dropped to her knees and grabbed his thumb, twisting it away from her body and causing the soldier to cry out in agony as his thumb and wrist were bent backwards.

She was free to run, but she did not want to. Aviv was fighting three soldiers, each moving warily around the strong and lithe warrior. Samson was almost unconscious on the cobbled stone alleyway with two soldiers tying his hands behind him with cord.

Aviv opened the throat of the man on his right easily, as the other two swung their swords and moved sideways to give themselves more room to move.

'Samson! Wake up!' Delilah ran to him, pushing one of the men behind him to the ground as she struck him with a short punch to the nose, another of Samson's latest training manoeuvres.

The man fell aside, blood streaming from his nose. 'Get that bitch under control before we have to kill her.' He looked at his hand and shuffled back away from her reach.

'Touch her and it will be you who dies.' Samson rallied at the idea of anything happening to Delilah. His hands were tied as he came to his knees and he strained on the bindings.

'I am sorry Samson.' Delilah cried as she ducked to avoid another assault from the first soldier who had attacked her. She knew he was unlikely to make the same mistake twice. Her time was running out. She felt as though a heavy weight had been laid on her shoulders.

Aviv smiled as he coaxed his two opponents forward. 'You sure you want to die today?' He held his dagger in his right hand, while encouraging them forward with a wave of his left.

'You are outnumbered,' one of the soldiers pointed out.

'Only until the big man over there breaks those bindings.' Both men looked tentatively to Samson who was flexing his muscles with a growl of frustration.

'Looks like he is having a little trouble.' The taller of the two soldiers laughed at his own jest.

'Sometimes you cannot rush these things.' Aviv shrugged and waited for the attack he knew would come.

The soldier with the foul-smelling breath grabbed Delilah again and as she cried out in fear and frustration Samson howled again. The man with the broken nose and his friend had a hold of Samson, one on each side but as the Nazarite let out his final frustration, the bindings creaked and broke, sending the two soldiers into the air. Both landed hard against either side of the alley and Aviv laughed.

'Time is up boys. Run or die. You choose.' Both men facing off against Aviv looked at each other as Samson took the man who had regained a hold of Delilah by the scruff of his neck, holding him aloft like a lioness would with a cub.

Aviv sheathed his dagger and raised his hands palm up with a final unspoken question and both men turned to run.

'Who sent you?' Samson growled as he violently shook the soldier he held.

The man's feet were far from the ground, his collar was choking him but still he refused to speak and Samson shook him harder. 'Do not be stubborn. I know the King wants me dead but did you really think these were going to hold me?'

The man looked from the broken bow strings in Samson's hand to Delilah and back again. *'You were wrong Delilah.'* The man's lips had not moved and his eyes were confused, as though he thought he knew something but then realised he had no idea at all.

There was no way for Delilah to respond to Dagon. A sudden sense of hopelessness enveloped her in that moment until the man Samson held began to mutter something.

'Dagon. The temple. The Priests. It was all of them.'

Samson looked confused at the soldier's declaration but when the man suddenly went blue in the face and his breathing became ragged, the big man dropped him to the ground.

He continued to gurgle until he convulsed and ceased to move at all.

Aviv walked over and gave him a kick. 'Is he dead?'

'He is, but I did not kill him.' Samson lifted his hands into the air as if to profess his innocence.

'You always underestimate your strength my friend.'

'No, really. I had let him go and he still strangled to death.'

Delilah was sitting on the floor, staring into the eye of the dead soldier. His tongue lolled out of his mouth and his eyes had bulged out of his skull, red and somehow inhuman.

Samson saw her begin to shake and lifted her from the cold stone alleyway. He felt more clear-headed, not entirely recovered, but more aware than earlier.

'Let us get you home Delilah.' Samson spoke softly as he scooped her up into his arms. She relaxed into the feeling of his warm body, relief instantly taking over.

'I am so sorry.' She kept saying every few moments.

'You have nothing to apologise for. It was my fault. I should have known better than to drink so much while you are with me. Your beauty brings all the animals out of the shadows.

'You do not understand.' Delilah tried to explain before weariness took over and she passed out on Samson's shoulder.

The two men walked on through the dark quiet streets until the estate came into view. The walk up the hill seemed longer than usual as both men were lost in their own thoughts.

Aviv took a deep breath and shared his concerns. 'You sure it was nothing to do with her Samson? That soldier said Dagon, the Temple and the Priests were all involved. They said she was to be unharmed before they attacked and where did we see her just the other night?'

'There is more to this Aviv. She fought to save me tonight. I agree that she knows something, more than she is letting on but she wanted to learn to fight for a reason. I do not believe it was because she feared the Priests would return to try and take her.'

Aviv nodded his understanding and patted his friend on the shoulder as they entered the gates of the estate.

Chapter 30

Delilah opened her eyes and stretched as the sun filtered through her bedroom window. For a moment, she was a young woman, welcoming a new day with the sweet smell of jasmine and the warmth of a summer morning. Then she suddenly remembered the previous night and a stab of pain in her chest threatened to stop her breathing.

Aggie appeared with a tray of flat bread, goat's-cheese and dried fruit and placed it on the side table before taking a seat on the edge of Delilah's bed.

'You slept well?' Asherah's eyes twinkled and Delilah studied them closely.

'What did you do?' Delilah asked as she took a sip of the fresh juice and scooped up some soft goat's-cheese with the flat bread.

'When Samson came with you last night, I helped him get you to bed. I could feel your anxiety child. I simply took it away, that and your dreams. You needed a good, solid night of sleep.'

Delilah touched her hand to Asherah's and felt the familiar tingle. 'What is that?'

'I emit an energy that you feel and absorb.' The goddess shrugged as though it were such a little thing.

'It is a wonderful feeling.' Delilah held her hand on the goddess's arm, savouring the feeling.

'What happened last night?' Asherah changed the subject effortlessly.

'I would rather not talk about it.' Delilah pushed her food aside as her appetite abandoned her.

'I am a goddess Delilah. I already know what happened. Telling me is for you to unburden yourself, not to receive my judgement.'

The young woman started to replay the events of the previous night in her mind. Asherah touched her arm and spoke quietly. 'You should not torture yourself. Samson is safe.'

'No thanks to me.' Delilah knew she was pouting like a child but she could not help herself.

'You fought well, but you also lied to Dagon. Samson's strength cannot be contained by binding him.'

'I honestly do not know where Samson's power comes from. He will not tell me. But if he does not tell me, Dagon will kill my family. He may already have. Are you sure you cannot save them?'

Asherah considered the girl's plight. 'We are not supposed to meddle.'

'I think you already have.' Delilah pointed out the obvious.

'Well, more importantly, we cannot directly interfere with the life and death of humanity. Believe me, I saved my people once and I was warned never to do something like that again.'

'Surely you can interfere indirectly? How does Dagon do it?'

Asherah considered the question. 'Dagon is a fallen angel. He does not have to play by the rules. He cannot be redeemed in the Creator's eyes.' The goddess finally touched Delilah's arm once more. 'Finish eating and go train with Samson. I will see what I can do.'

****

Samson began his training minus Aviv and Delilah. Their absence did not worry him and after last night, he hardly expected to see Delilah, and Aviv had never proven himself the most reliable training partner.

'Why does a strong man like you need to train anyway?' The estate guards had taken turns sparring with Samson, warily at first, but they were growing more confident.

'Strength is not everything. Training hones the reflexes, teaches muscle memory and sharpens my ability to read my opponents.' Samson explained as he blocked an expected lunge and knocked the guard's sword clear of his hand.

The remaining guards hollered and clapped as the sword landed ten paces from the sparring pair, right amongst the garden beds that surrounded the grounds.

'Just like that.' Samson nodded to the flower bed, then waved his sword in the direction of the next man lined up to take on the Israelite champion.

'I think it is my turn now.' Delilah smiled as Samson turned his attention to the sweet sound of her voice.

'Delilah. I expected you to skip training and take a day of rest.'

'Rest is for the wicked, or so they say.' Delilah winked shyly.

'And you are not wicked Delilah?' Samson walked toward her and left the group of guards smiling and jesting behind him.

'Are you sure you are alright?' Samson moved close to look deep into Delilah's eyes. She looked back at his intense stare, finally blinking to distract herself.

'Yes. I am. I was worried about you though.'

'Me!' Samson almost laughed. 'I am probably the last man you need to worry about. My gift keeps me safe Delilah.'

'Well forgive me if I do not put the same faith in your gift or your god as you do.'

'About that.' Samson stopped as Delilah put up her hand and pulled her dagger from the scabbard.

'Training first. Talks of gods and goddesses later.'

'Goddesses? I never said anything about goddesses.' Samson frowned.

'Later!' Delilah swung her dagger around her wrist as she had seen Samson and Aviv do many times before. Samson tried not to grin but he failed. He walked away from Delilah towards a stand of practice swords.

'Where are you going?' Delilah let the dagger drop to her side, her voice rising an octave as she stormed after him indignantly.

'Here, take this.' Samson threw a wooden sword at the young woman who caught it with her left hand, her right still fully occupied with her dagger. 'Nice.' Samson observed. 'Have you always been able to use both hands equally?'

Delilah studied the two weapons in her hands, the left then the right and returned her gaze to the Nazarite. 'I think so.'

'Then this might be more fun than I thought.'

Chapter 31

Aviv was no saint and he knew his own chequered past may well come back to haunt him, but Samson was his one and only friend and there was something not right about his situation with Delilah.

He left the estate early, missing training to meet up with some associates and see if he could find out more about Delilah's past. He had a niggling feeling that started shortly after dawn and would not leave him.

He had always given the religious zealots a wide berth, preferring to instil his trust in the more reliable power of the cities. The Thieve's Guild and he were not exactly on speaking terms, but Samson's life and even Delilah's when he thought about it, meant more to him than his own; which was a realisation that made the man chuckle to himself.

'What are you smirking about Aviv?' The burly bouncer with his bare tattooed arms and heavy hand-carved baton frowned as he puffed up his chest and barred Aviv's way.

'What, smirking has been outlawed by the Guild? I had no idea Brutus. When did that happen?' Aviv feigned shock and the guard shook his head.

'That lip of yours will see you without hands, or better still, without a tongue if you do not watch your mouth.'

Aviv bowed royally and winked at the guard. 'Is she in?'

'Yes, she is in, but she will not be happy to see you mind.'

'I do not believe you, Katya is always happy to see me.' Aviv patted his chest with the palm of his hand and pursed his lips. The guard mumbled something incoherent as he unbolted the bar that kept intruders away.

Aviv ducked through the low doorway and moved down the narrow corridor. At the end, two more guards waited, hands on their sword hilts as he approached. As he met the gaze of the taller of the two guards, with his hand outstretched, Aviv nodded his understanding and unbuckled his sword and handed it over.

The guard did not move, he waited patiently and indicated with his eyes to Aviv's groin.

The merchant shrugged and removed the small baldric he kept in a sheath strapped to his thigh.

'Good memory Bashar. I would never use it you know. It is just an old friend that keeps me company. You know how it is.'

Bashar raised an eyebrow but stepped aside as Aviv reluctantly gave up his 'old friend'.

He took a deep breath before entering the lioness's den and pasted a long-lost smile on his face.

The room was well lit with torches alight along every wall, spaced out evenly with expensive artworks and ornate rugs hanging perfectly straight. Katya sat on the soft silk divan with her immaculately manicured fingers and toes and not a hair out of place.

Aviv's smile turned to an involuntary grin as his eyes followed Katya's rather exposed long, lean and bronzed leg all the way up to the revealing split at the top of her sheer skirt.

'Impressive as always Katya.' Aviv bowed, keeping a respectful distance.

'Nice to see some things never change. I assume you are desperate Aviv or I cannot imagine why you would show your face here again.'

'Water under the bridge Katya. Surely we have grown up and moved on from our past?' Aviv rose from his bow and held his hands in mock pleading.

'There is not a lot of water or bridges around here in case you have failed to notice Aviv.'

'I am sorry Katya. Truly I am. I was young, new to the life and I will repay my debt, right down to the last copper. I just need some information and I would not have come if it was not important.'

Katya seemed to consider the merchant's plea. She was flanked by two personal body guards, one of whom stepped forward to whisper something in her ear.

Katya looked fondly at the man and nodded, returning her gaze to Aviv. 'I understand you have found a friend in your new legitimate life. Let us see if we can strike a deal, one that you might actually honour this time.'

Aviv frowned and considered his options. He had already come too far to go back and the information he sought, only Katya could procure. He looked from Katya to the whispering body guard and noted the sneer on the man's face and the gleam in his eye. He was a seasoned warrior and one to match Aviv. Then there was still the other guard and Katya herself, who was formidable on her own.

The merchant weighed his choice and decided he had known the moment he entered the den that he had none. Katya had him right where she wanted him, but he needed to be there.

'What deal did you have in mind Katya?'

'Your friend is powerful, both in his role as a Judge and his strength is renowned. Let us just say that when the time comes that I need one of his powers, you will ensure he is at my disposal.'

Aviv took a deep breath and considered the deal. 'Very well. I am sure I can convince Samson that the needs outweigh the inconvenience, however I will say one thing, there is no way on this earth that I can force Samson to do anything, so it will have to be something that does not put at risk his faith, or his people. Against his enemies, I am sure he will do whatever I ask.'

Katya pursed her lips for added tension and then allowed a grin to spread across her mouth. 'I have nothing against the Israelites, so I can see that will not inhibit my needs. Very well. What is it you need Aviv?'

'May I take a seat?' Aviv indicated the cushion near the table by Katya's divan. She opened her hand and invited him to sit. He removed his sandals and approached the queen of the Thieves Guild of Gaza and took his place at her feet. He resisted the temptation to massage her feet as he once would have and closed off the rising desire before he betrayed himself but he was too slow. Katya placed a grape in her mouth and licked her lips seductively.

Aviv cleared his throat. 'My friend and I have taken a Sorek local girl into our care.' Katya raised an eyebrow and Aviv waved her accusations away. 'She was stealing for the temple and instead of charging her, Samson decided to help her. The point is, she is behaving strangely and let us say that Samson has enemies, particular in Gaza who wish him harm.'

Katya laughed aloud. 'The strongest man alive and he can be harmed!'

'So far no, but that does not stop his enemies from trying to ascertain the source of his strength.'

'There is a source?'

Aviv was treading on sinking sand and he needed to survive. 'That is not relevant. The girl is acting strangely and we need to know more about her background in Sorek.'

'And you want me to ask my sources in Sorek?'

'I would be eternally grateful.' Aviv bowed his head and Katya leant forward and ran her fingers through his hair. Aviv fought the urge rising in his chest. He took a deep breath and calmed himself against her touch.

'I have missed you Aviv.' Katya dragged on his hair forcing the merchant to look up. He took Katya's hand in his and brought it to his lips, kissing each finger slowly and gently, savouring her taste and the look in her eyes.

The whispering bodyguard moved forward but Katya put her free hand up in the air and pointed for him to leave.

The man snarled audibly but did as his mistress ordered, taking the remaining guard with him.

Katya took a tighter grasp of Aviv's hair and coaxed him to join her on the divan. The merchant needed little encouragement and took his lead from the woman who once used the same hand to order him, just as she ordered the snarling bodyguard.

Chapter 32

Aviv had made himself scarce over the last few days, but Samson was not complaining. His new training partner was proving to be a quick study and she was far more attractive.

'That is it! Now draw the bow-string back gently and steady your aim with your thumb on your cheek. Perfect.' Samson looked over Delilah's shoulder at her mark. 'You have a good eye.'

Delilah did not smile; even a grin could alter her aim. Instead, she took a breath, a final aim and released. The thud of the arrow striking the wood and straw dummy was exciting and sent tingles down Delilah's spine or was it the proximity of Samson, breathing soft warm breaths down her back?

The sun was getting low in the sky and as Delilah turned around to return her bow to the rack she caught the look in Samson's eyes. It mirrored her own. Samson touched her cheek softly at first until Delilah turned her lips to kiss his hand.

Samson responded by taking the bow from her hands and dropping it to the ground. He wrapped his arm around her waist and pulled her close. Delilah lifted her face to meet his and Samson brushed her cheek with his lips.

'I think I had better take you back to Aggie.'

'I do not need a chaperone Samson. I am a big girl now.' Delilah reached up behind Samson's head and pulled his lips back to meet hers. This time, the Nazarite did not fight his rising passion.

****

Jud had no idea why the mistress wanted to know about some Temple whore but he was not paid to think. He was paid to get information. He had asked around discreetly but very few people in Sorek knew anything useful about Delilah. Jud had been watching her parents for a few days now and he was not the only one.

The Temple soldier was terrible at the work. He chose the same place to watch the house. He followed the father each day as he left to run errands. What Jud did not understand was why the Temple was watching the girl's family. If she was a whore, then why watch her family? If she was to be a virgin sacrifice, again there was no need to watch her family.

He avoided the main thoroughfare as he made his way back to his home. He dodged a homeless beggar, throwing a coin in the man's basket as he took the stairs to his rooftop terrace. The pigeons were quiet until he reached inside to retrieve one. They scattered but Jud found his favourite and drew him out of the cage.

He wrapped the note around the bird's leg and clipped it in place with the cuff. He held the wings in place until he reached the edge of the roof top and gently released the bird into flight. It knew where it was heading and the Mistress would have his assumptions by nightfall.

****

'I missed you Katya. I wish I could go back and change the past.'

'That is a lie Aviv. You were infatuated then and you still are. You have the attention span of a two-year-old.' Katya softened her words with a smile as she leaned forward and kissed Aviv firmly on the lips.

'You wound me.' Aviv clutched his chest as Katya allowed him to take a breath.

'There is no need to flatter me my friend. I have enjoyed the last few days with you but I have no need for a husband. Husbands are for weak women who have no financial means of their own, women like your Delilah.

'She is Samson's Delilah, not mine.'

'You sound upset about that.'

Aviv shrugged as he considered Katya. Was he upset that Delilah was to be Samson's, eventually? 'I guess I could do worse.' Aviv laughed aloud as he drew Katya down on to his bare chest. She swung her dark locks over her shoulder and stared into Aviv's eyes, teasing him with their sparkle.

'You like her?'

'I have no intentions of taking a wife Katya. As you said, I have a very short attention span.' Aviv lifted Katya's face to his and began to kiss the queen of the Thieves Guild passionately.

He drew her closer and began to untie the bodice of her dress, the heat in his groin rising yet again. 'Three days and you still have energy. I am impressed.' Katya teased.

A knock on the door drew a curse from Aviv as Katya retied her bodice and shooed Aviv to the other end of the divan.

'Enter!' A guard opened the door, approached Katya and held out the tiniest piece of parchment Aviv had ever seen.

'Thank you. There will be no need for a reply. Put the bird away with the others.'

The guard bowed and left the room without a comment.

'What is that?' Aviv moved closer once the door was closed, his hand absently playing with Katya's laces.

'A message from one of my informants in Sorek. News of your lady friend.' Katya winked.

'Samson's lady friend. I keep telling you. What does it say?' Aviv sat upright, all thought of Katya's bodice forgotten.

Katya opened the little note and read it quickly. Aviv could see only a few symbols on the parchment and frowned his confusion.

'A code.' Katya explained briefly. 'It says your friend's family are being watched by the Temple and he does not seem to think it is a beneficial service on the Priest's part.'

'That would make sense.' Aviv frowned as he thought through the options.

'It would?'

'Either Delilah is an informant for the Temple and the soldiers are watching to keep her family safe or she is working for them unwillingly, and her parents are the Temple's bargaining chip.'

'What do you believe is more likely?'

Aviv took a deep breath and considered Delilah and what little he knew of her. Samson was an accident. She did not steal from him intentionally and she had no idea Samson would take her to Gaza and not simply hand her over to the authorities.

'She is unwilling and they are hostages.'

'Can I do anything?'

'I need to let Samson know. I do not think it is wise to make the Temple soldiers aware that we know, so do nothing for now, but I might call in a favour later if you think I have still earned it.' Aviv grinned and Katya slapped him affectionately on the arm.

'I have not decided yet. I will let you know in the morning.' Aviv smiled and began to untie Katya's bodice once more.

Chapter 33

'She is working for Dagon and the Philistines.' Aviv spoke in hushed tones in the corner of the courtyard. 'Against her will.'

Samson released the breath he had taken when Aviv first mentioned Delilah's betrayal. 'My friend. I knew something was not right. Poor Delilah.'

'What information is she to share with the Philistines then?'

'How to kill me I suspect.'

'The attack in the alley?'

'Probably.' Samson nodded.

'Has she asked you again what gives you your strength?'

'No. I need to let her know we can keep her family safe.'

'Can we?'

'I hope so. Your friend. Can she help?'

'Against the Philistines and all the Dagon temple soldiers, I am not sure Samson.'

Samson rubbed his chin and took a deep breath. 'Leave this between you and me for now Aviv.'

Aviv nodded reluctantly. 'What are you going to do?'

Samson had not time to answer as Delilah walked into the courtyard to join them for dinner. Aggie walked beside her, carrying a platter of cooked meat, flatbread and green salad.

'That smells delicious.' Samson rose and helped Aggie with the platter. He placed it down on the table and turned to kiss Delilah gently on the cheek.

'Did I miss something?' Aviv shook his head as though he were waking himself from a deep sleep.

Delilah laughed, a musical tone that sent tingling sensations down Aviv's spine.

'Depends my friend. What did you say your old friend's name was? Katya?'

'Well, I did not miss that of course Samson, but what did I miss here?'

Samson wrapped his arm around Delilah and smiled in a way Aviv had never seen before. Their earlier conversation flooded back to him. Samson was infatuated with Delilah before, was he in love with her now?

****

'Asherah is meddling Dagon.' Moloch paced as he spun a gold chain around in circles until it wound around his finger and stopped with a charm—a star surrounded by a circle—on top of his finger.

'I know brother. I cannot get through the barrier she has erected around Delilah.' Dagon stood in the form of Kaamill, his embroidered robes sparking in the dim candlelight of the vestibule.

'Then how are you to find a way to kill Samson?' Moloch unwound his charm, before spinning it once more

'I am working on possible solutions.' Dagon found the angel's obsession with the symbol infuriating, but kept his opinions to himself. Moloch was his only ally.

'You could kill her mother.' Moloch offered absentmindedly as he studied the charm on his finger.

'That would be a waste of resources brother. If I cannot share such a threat with her, it would hold no bargaining power. I need to get a message to her, one that she will have no choice but to act on.'

'If you had not sacrificed her friend, you might have been able to utilise her services.'

'Killing her was a threat in itself and it worked.'

'It did not work. She gave you false information.' Moloch stared accusingly at his brother.

'Yes, and that disturbs me Moloch. Why would she do that when I could kill her parents?'

'Maybe she cares more for the Nazarite than her family?' Moloch spun the charm back around his finger until it once more dangled from the long gold chain.

'What are you doing with that?' Dagon allowed his frustration to rise. 'You have not stopped fiddling with it all this time.'

'It is a gift.' Moloch shrugged as though that explained everything.

'A gift from whom?'

'Astarte.'

'Is she still infatuated with you?' Moloch thought about it a moment and nodded. 'Then we can possibly distract Asherah with Astarte. She is not going to be lead astray by you again.'

'I am not happy to use Astarte like that.'

'No time to be sentimental brother. Heaven is at stake.'

'I am not sure the life or death of the Nazarite is worth the sacrifice of our brethren!'

'He is father's symbol, a beacon of hope for their eternity. We kill the invincible Samson and the Creator's power is questioned, therefore his prophecy for the Prince of Peace is broken.'

****

The moon was high and there was a slight coolness to the evening. The scent of jasmine hung in the air and the sound of crunching gravel echoed across the courtyard as Delilah walked with Samson.

'Do you still need to stay here Samson? Gaza is a dangerous place for an Israelite. Why do we not return to my home, or travel to your home?' Delilah snuggled into Samson's embrace and shivered.

'Are you cold?'

'No, just a little frightened for you.' Delilah stopped and looked up into Samson's eyes.

'I understand your fear, but the Philistine King plans to enslave my people Delilah. Your father was privy to plans before he left and now that he has shared his knowledge with me, I cannot simply leave until I understand how and can stop him'

Delilah wrapped her arms around Samson's neck, reaching up to kiss his lips gently. 'Oh Samson.

Why do the Philistines and Israelites hate each other so much? My father and mother seemed to love each other regardless of their faith or origins.'

'The Philistines worship Dagon. They are heathens who have a lawless society.'

'But they have music and culture like nothing I have ever seen before.'

'Distractions.' Samson removed Delilah's arms from his neck and held her hands as he studied her face.

'Distractions from what?'

'From the cause of Yahweh.'

'Oh Samson, we were not born to fight and die for a mighty creator. We were born to live and love, let Yahweh use all his godly power to do his own work.' Delilah made to kiss Samson, but he pulled back with a frown of confusion.

'I *am* a Nazarite Delilah, sworn to serve Yahweh with all the power and strength he has given me.' He let Delilah's hands drop and she allowed the distance to grow between them.

'Serve in what way? Killing Philistines? Surely if Yahweh wanted to kill off all the Philistines he would do so with a plague or a famine?'

'It is never that simple. We all have a purpose to serve and we are given the power to do so, Nazarites even more so.'

Delilah realised there was no way she was going to be able to get Samson to leave this fight for others. He was a passionate man who believed wholeheartedly in his cause.

Instead, she took his hands in hers and turned to face the Nazarite. 'Just ignore me Samson. I am only worried that something might happen to you.'

Samson swung her around gently to face the starlit sky. He wrapped his arm around her slim waist and pulled her close to his chest burying his face in her hair. The smell of her warm skin was exhilarating.

He kissed her neck gently nuzzling, coaxing her to relax into his embrace. He pulled her close and whispered into her ear.

'You must give the temple what they seek Delilah. Better now, while your family is still safe.'

Delilah stiffened in his embrace and swung around to face him with fear and shock in her eyes. Samson dragged her into his body tightly and kissed her before she could say a word.

 **Chapter 34**

Delilah went to the window and raised the candle as instructed. She sank to the floor of her room and leant against the wall, blowing out the candle as if the darkness would hide both her pain and her shame.

The sound of clashing swords drifted to her senses and she finally drew herself up to find a strength she did not know she possessed.

In the darkness, she found her bow and a quiver of arrows right where she had left them. She had promised Samson she would not enter into the fight, but sitting on the battlements taking shots at Dagon's soldiers was not exactly joining the fight.

She smiled as she ran down the corridor, to the end where the spiral staircase wound its way up to the battlement above the courtyard. The soldiers would need to travel through this well-lit area to get to Samson's room. The first one broke clear of Aviv and his guards and began to run across the clearing. Delilah loosened a shaft that took him in the throat, knocking him from his feet.

Aviv looked over his shoulder to discover the source of the thud and smiled. He returned his attention to a Temple soldier who was easily a head taller than he.

The man ran at Aviv, a growl emanating for his chest as he swung his sword recklessly. Aviv grinned at the lack of skill and stepped aside. The energy behind the soldier kept him moving past his target and Aviv stepped in to stab his enemy through the lower back. He still had a hold of the man's collar when another opponent swung a wild attack his way. He spun the now dead soldier around to take the blow, dropped him to the ground, retrieving his sword from the man's back and fluidly taking the head off his new attacker.

Delilah watched Aviv fight and could not help but wonder where a merchant had gained the skill, but Aviv had a past he was unwilling to share. She knew now that she understood where Samson's information about her family had come from.

The battle continued and each man who cleared the fray, found another of Delilah's arrows, but her quiver was now empty. Aviv signalled his men to retreat as planned and waved to Delilah.

For a moment, she could not move. In retreating she felt as though she was letting these men take Samson. She had no real choice but to do Dagon's bidding, but now, now she felt as though she had a choice, the choice to fight to save him from capture.

As if reading her thoughts Aviv appeared on the battlement alongside her. 'Time to go Delilah.' He waved for her to join him.

Delilah remained rooted to the spot. 'I cannot abandon him Aviv.'

'It is done Delilah. This is not about you now. This is Samson's journey.' Aviv grabbed the young woman by the wrist and lifted her to her feet. 'I promised him Delilah. Do not make me break my promise.'

Delilah looked up and nodded. She swung her bow over her shoulder and with a heavy heart, followed Aviv to safety.

Chapter 35

Samson opened his eyes to the darkness and groaned as he took a deep breath, his ribs creaking with the effort. The feeling was foreign. Pain was something other men experienced at his hand.

'The Nazarite still breathes.' King Dawsar stepped forward and punched Samson in the chest. The explosion of air was accompanied by a grunt of pain and the King smiled at the accomplishment.

'I told you Delilah would come through.' A young and tall man Samson had never seen before stepped into the damp cell with a torch in his hand. He placed it carefully in the wall socket and as he turned, Samson glimpsed his eyes. They were not the eyes of a young man, they had seen and felt more than a lifetime, Samson knew.

'Yes, great warrior of Yahweh. How does it feel to be deceived by the woman you love?' The king lifted Samson's head by his shortly cropped hair and laughed. 'Your long locks are gone my friend and your days of terrorising my men are over.'

'Just kill me and be done with it Dawsar.' Samson's voice croaked with the effort. He had no idea how long he had been in the King's dungeon, but he was growing weaker from thirst and hunger.

'Kill you! What kind of example to your people would it be to simply kill you quietly while no one is watching? I have plans for you.'

'Then you had better feed me and give me water or I will surely die before you fulfil them.'

'He is right my Lord. If you are to keep him alive until the harvest festival, then you should feed him.' The tall man in the long robes with the golden thread and high collar spoke again.

Samson continued to study the stranger through swollen eyes. He wore ornate robes that Samson had never seen. He was older than he looked and he bore a confidence that belied his stature. He decided he was in no position to really care now and pushed the thought from his mind.

'Very well, bring him water and some food. Not too much mind.'

'What will you do with him now?'

'Send him to grind grain at the mill. He might not be invincible, but he is still strong enough to work.'

The two men casually left the cell as though beating prisoners in dungeons were a common pastime. Both took one last look before the King removed the torch from the wall and retreated leaving Samson in the darkness.

The Nazarite was relieved to be left alone with his pain. His heart ached for Delilah and he hoped that Aviv and his men were not harmed when the temple soldiers came for him.

He recalled the tears streaking down Delilah's face as she cut his hair. With every handful that fell on the stone floor, she had shuddered. The memory of the softness of her touch filled him with courage now. It had been the only way and Yahweh would forgive him for breaking his vow to never cut his hair.

It is not your hair that binds you to the Creator Samson, it is your heart.

The voice was gentle and encouraging and Samson laughed as he began to believe the confinement had already brought madness upon him.

****

It had been days since Delilah had been in this room. She collapsed to the ground as she attempted to pick up the broken pieces of the vase from Samson's night stand. Her heart pounded as she recalled the night they came for him.

Samson had insisted she not stay in his room, that the danger was too great and she had agreed to leave him. Samson had touched her cheek and pulled her lovingly to him. The feeling of his strong body against hers was something she clung to now.

Tears sprang to her eyes as she remembered cutting his hair. It felt like each cut was taking a piece of him with it. They had sat on his balcony, watching the hair land on the stone, then fly away with the breeze.

When Samson had told her that she must give the Philistines what they wanted she had argued and refused but then he had told her that both her and her parents' lives were in danger and he would not have the possibility of her death on his shoulders. It was too much for him to bear.

Aviv had reduced the guard to minimise casualties. He was not happy about the prospect of giving up without a real fight, but Samson had been adamant that they would take him, so why risk lives in the process?

Samson had been tied before the men came. That was what Dagon had demanded and Delilah had done what was asked of her. As she tied the ropes around her lover's hands she had begged him for forgiveness.

His words racked her with pain now. 'There is nothing to forgive my love.' But there was. If she had never met Samson, never stolen his coin purse, never been such a brat to her parents then none of this would have happened.

'What are you doing Delilah?' Aggie dropped to her knees to help the young woman up. 'Put down the broken vase, you will cut yourself.'

'I want to die Aggie.' Delilah wanted to call her Asherah, to beg the goddess for forgiveness but she could not bring herself to ask. After everything she had done, she did not deserve the love of the gods.

Aggie looked at Delilah, the broken pottery poised above her delicate soft wrist. 'Nonsense child. Get up. Samson is not yet dead.' She coaxed the broken shard from the girl's hands and lifted her to her feet.

Aggie was right. No announcement had been made, in fact the King had not even told the people he had the last Judge of Israel in his dungeon. Delilah was suddenly curious. 'Why has the King not gloated to his own people or the Israelites?'

'He plans to make a spectacle of Samson's death—an example to the Israelites not to fight against Philistine rule. He wants them submissive and what better way than to publicly execute the man of strength, Yahweh's champion?'

'This is all my fault.' Delilah forced herself not to cry. She had no idea why she was so emotional. Yes, Samson was in prison, but she felt like a flood of tears could start and never stop.

'Oh Delilah, none of this is your fault. You are like all your brethren, at the mercy of powers you do not know or understand.'

'What do you mean?' Delilah took a deep breath to bring her emotions under control.

'Dagon, me, Yahweh. There is a place beyond what you know that you cannot begin to understand. Games are played child and although you make your own choices, your circumstances are never within your control.'

Delilah knew of the gods of course. She, more than anyone understood what Aggie was saying. She knew Dagon personally. Not everyone is chosen to be queen to a dark angel.

'You mean this was all orchestrated? By whom?'

'By Dagon, by me and to an extent by the Creator himself.' Asherah could see Delilah's features change, as though such a realisation had not come to her before but now that it had, nothing would ever be the same again.

'So let me understand you correctly. There are gods, many gods and you all play games with us and our lives?'

'No Delilah it is not that simple. Yes, there are what you might call gods but we are not gods, we are eternal yes but there is only one Creator and he created us as much as he created you.'

'You live forever and we do not, that makes you gods in anyone's book.'

Asherah wanted so much to share the prophecy with Delilah but it was forbidden. Only the angels knew of Yahweh's plan and it was causing war amongst them. If the humans knew of the eternal realm and considered it attainable—what would they do to grasp it with their own hands? The goddess hated to consider it. Their time would come, it was written.

'My point is Samson is alive and Dagon is working with the Philistines to undermine the Israelites. It suits his purposes right now.'

'And you are working with the Israelites?' Delilah raised an eyebrow in question.

'Not exactly.' Asherah considered her words carefully. 'My people are not the Israelites or the Philistines. I once had my own people but they are now scattered and I honestly have no need to be labelled as the goddess of a particular ethnicity. I love humans Delilah, each and every one of them, and watching them fight each other and die, tears at my heart.'

'So, you manipulate to avoid death, while Dagon plays games to bring death?' Delilah's conclusion seemed to click in her mind and she rose from the shattered crockery like a phoenix from fire. 'I need to find Aviv. I need to get my family to safety.'

Chapter 36

'Can I see him Aviv? Have you managed to find a way to get me in to see him?'

'It was difficult but Katya has a man, a guard in the prison. I am not sure you should see him Delilah. They are transferring him to the work-mill soon and it will be easier for us to get to him there, but he has been beaten. It will only distress you to see him now.'

'Stop it Aviv. I put him there; I have to accept that how I find him is my own fault.'

'Delilah, you did not put him there, he chose his own journey. He could have killed every damned one of them, but he chose you.'

'Exactly. One way or another I caused this mess. I aim to fix it. I need to see him, to tell him what I am doing.' Delilah's nostrils flared and her hands were on her hips. She knew no other way but to be angry. If she did not stay angry, she would fall apart.

'I will make the arrangements.' Aviv touched her arm and Delilah pulled away reflexively.

'Good. Now what about my parents?'

'They are safe for now. The Temple soldiers continue to watch them though.' Aviv studied Delilah closely, gauging his words carefully.

'We leave the day after I see Samson. I want my family moved Aviv. Somewhere Dagon will never find them.'

'You mean the Temple soldiers will never find them?' Aviv frowned his confusion.

'No Aviv. I mean Dagon.'

'Are you alright Delilah? Dagon is a non-existent god that the local people worship because they are not smart enough to know gods are how kings control peasants.' The merchant frowned as Delilah smiled and shook her head.

'I think it might be time you had a good talk with Aggie.'

Aviv looked Delilah up and down as though she were heading for madness. He had known she was grieving and using anger to mask her pain, but this was delusional. 'What has Aggie to do with the temple of Dagon?'

'Come with me and I will show you.' Delilah walked toward the cook-house and almost bumped into Aggie in the doorway.

'Just the person I needed to see.' Delilah indicated that Aviv should follow her. She gently collected Aggie's arm as she walked into the cook-house, past the long preparation table and hearth and down to the rear where servants usually took their meals.

A small wooden table surrounded by benches stood in the corner. Delilah waved her hand for Aviv to take a seat and smiled at Aggie's questioning gaze. 'You too.' Delilah helped Aggie into the rickety bench seat and took the seat alongside.

'What do you need Delilah?' Aggie continued in her old gruff voice, maintaining her disguise but not her composure.

'If I am to save my family, Samson and myself, you need to answer my questions truthfully for Aviv here.'

Aggie suddenly realised what was coming and pleaded. 'Delilah, there are some things I am not at liberty to share.'

'This is not Samson you are sharing with. Aviv is no zealot for any god, in fact he thinks the gods are all myth devised to keep the poor under control.'

Aggie smiled knowingly. 'You knew I would not like such an accusation.'

'I did.' Delilah smiled triumphantly. 'Now tell him who you really are, no, actually, I think you should show him. I have not seen the real you either and I am intrigued.'

Aviv looked from Delilah to Aggie and back again. His faced was full of apprehension but his curiosity was piqued.

'You are right, Samson would struggle with this wisdom but I believe Aviv will cope.' Aggie's hand moved in circles and a stream of light began to appear on her fingertips.

Aviv gasped and fell back on his wobbly bench, almost losing his balance as the servant before him shimmered like the setting sun on an oasis of water. As the bright light disappeared from her hands and her face, Aviv could see a young and beautiful woman before him. Her hair was long and golden and her eyes a sparkling blue. Her skin was the colour of clouds, accentuated by the teal colour dress she now wore.

'Who are you?' Aviv forced his mouth shut and felt the rising need for a stiff drink.

'My name is Asherah, Aviv. I am what you might call a goddess.'

'Just as Dagon is a god, a real and tangible dangerous vile god who wants Samson dead and me as his bride.' Delilah finished in a rush of fury.

Aviv nodded to Delilah's statement but could not drag his eyes from Asherah. 'How is this possible?'

'Well that is a story I have no intention of explaining. I like this body much better Delilah. I think I will keep it.'

'This is not the real you?' Aviv spoke but failed to close his mouth once more when he was finished.

'It is and it is not. I can be whoever I want to be.'

'Now that would come in handy.' Aviv grinned and the trance was finally broken. 'Dagon wants you as his bride. No wonder he wanted Samson out of the way. The only man on earth who had any chance of standing up to a god and he is in love with you too. Now because of his love, he is powerless to protect you from Dagon.' A sudden thought came to the merchant. 'What about you Asherah, can you kill Dagon?'

'No one can kill Dagon, only the Creator can and I do not believe he would.' Asherah patted Aviv on the arm and the tingle of energy made him shiver.

'Who is the Creator?' Aviv looked more confused than ever.

'Yahweh from all accounts.' Delilah explained and Asherah nodded her agreement.

'So what can you do? Can you get Samson out of prison?'

'I am afraid not. I am meddling enough by simply revealing my identity to you and Delilah. There is a prophecy that shows Samson bringing down Dagon's temple, but that will not kill Dagon.'

'It will disrupt the Philistines for a while though.' Aviv smiled.

'True enough.' Asherah's eyes grew momentarily sad. 'But to bring down the Temple he must stay in prison and that will cost him dearly.'

'What have you seen?' Delilah moved closer to Asherah and pleaded for her honesty with her eyes.

'I have seen Samson in great pain Delilah but the temple will fall. It is his destiny.'

'And what is my destiny without the man that should be my husband by my side?'

'Your destiny is yet to be fully revealed.'

Chapter 37

The wait had been agonising but finally Katya's man was on duty. He opened the gates to the lower dungeon of the King's castle and Delilah wrapped her hood tightly around her face. Aviv took her arm and led her through the darkness.

The guard collected a torch from the corridor wall and handed it to Aviv. He moved on without a word and Aviv followed, the torch held out and aloft to light the way.

The smell of stale urine and mouldy hay was heavy in the air and Delilah fought the urge to purge her stomach. 'Are you well?' Aviv whispered.

'As well as can be expected. You were right. This is horrible.'

They walked on in silence, reaching the very last cell at the deepest darkest corner of the lowest level. The temperature was so cool this far down that Delilah's breath misted into the air like smoke.

The guard unlocked the final cell and Delilah's breathing quickened. She felt physically ill and shivered with anticipation. Would Samson even be alive?

The man hanging from the shackles on the wall was limp. His face was swollen and his body was covered in welts that had already begun to fester.

'Samson.' Delilah whimpered as his name left her lips. 'What have I done?'

Aviv grabbed Delilah's arms as she rushed past him, her hood thrown back, her eyes wet with unshed tears. 'Approach slowly, he may not be himself right now.'

Delilah slowed her pace and took another few steps. 'Samson. Can you hear me?'

The man looked up and recognition shone through the bruised and battered eye slits. 'I thought I was dreaming your voice in my head.' He managed a smile that cracked his already broken lip, leaving a trickle of blood.

Delilah touched his face, gently dabbing the blood away with the sleeve of her cloak. 'I am getting my family out Samson, away from the Temple soldiers. You can use your strength to be free of this place.'

Samson shook his head. 'No, my strength has left me with my broken vow.'

'Your hair is but a symbol of your vow Samson. You are still gifted by Yahweh. Trust me. I need two days to get my family away and then you can be free of this place.' Delilah looked around the dark stone walls and supressed a shudder.

'You do not understand. I have seen this place in my dreams. I am to stay here Delilah and serve my God as he sees fit.'

'This is madness. The Philistines will kill you and if you die, I die Samson.'

'Take her Aviv. Do not bring her back here.' Samson stared past Delilah's pleading eyes to his friend who nodded his understanding.

'It will be as you say Samson.'

'No! Samson, no, please do not do this.' Aviv moved forward as Delilah's voice became hysterical.

'Stay quiet Delilah or we all die.' The whispered truth struck a cord and Delilah fought the urge to let her fear and pain turn to anger.

The walk back along the corridor felt like a lifetime. Delilah blinked her eyes closed as the sunlight burnt her vision, leaving sun spots that sparkled before her. She lifted her hood back over her face and followed Aviv without truly seeing anything around her.

The numbness spread throughout her body until her legs threatened to give way. She took a deep breath and forced herself to think of her parents. She needed to focus on them now. She could do nothing to save Samson, his mind was made up. He was ready to die for his cause, or for her, or for whatever stupid martyrdom he revered, but her parents were innocent in all of this mess.

Once her family was safe, she would go to Dagon and make a bargain with him, one he could not possibly refuse.

****

'Time to put you to work.' The guard unshackled one of Samson's hands warily and bound it to the other before unshackling the second from the wall.

Samson shuffled forward with both hands tied together and his feet joined by short chains that allowed only for small movements. Another guard grabbed him roughly and pushed him ahead.

'I still think they should just kill him for all the men *he* has murdered.'

'Well that is not your call is it!' The first guard argued.

'They said we could not kill him, no one said anything about getting retribution for the fallen. My cousin died by his hand. I owe it to my family to make it right.'

The first guard seemed to waver slightly and the second considered that permission. As Samson moved into the corridor that led to the remaining cells, the guard with the vendetta grabbed Samson by his shortened hair and forced his face down onto a stone block.

Samson had heard of how the Philistines tortured their enemies and he was not afraid of pain, but something told him this was going to be different. The first guard seemed unsure, but tied Samson's hands to the large rings that were mounted below the stone.

'Get the hot poker from the fire will you?' The guard ordered the first after he tied Samson down.

'I really think this is a bad idea. The king might not be too happy to have his prize sacrifice damaged.'

'What will he care? Hold his head still.'

The first guard forced Samson's face down on the stone. Samson fought the man but his strength was still gone from him and the man restrained him easily.

'That is it, now you will understand the pain and suffering you have caused you piece of dung.'

Samson could see the hot iron as it approached his eye. He wanted to shut his eyes but he knew closing off the vison would not make the guard stop.

In his soul, he wondered if he might in fact deserve the punishment.

He had served Yahweh faithfully for many years. Some said it was Yahweh who had led him to his first wife, to show that marrying out of his culture would only end in pain. But it was not Yahweh who had enraged him into killing so many Philistines for revenge.

He was a violent man until he met Delilah. She had found in him a softness he never knew existed. Since her, killing had not seemed so easy; serving Yahweh, even more difficult. This was his chance to make amends.

The iron touched his eye but there was no pain. The guard forced the hot iron deeper, trying desperately to elicit a cry from the Nazarite but none came.

'The other eye.' The guard barked and the first soldier did as he was ordered. He lifted Samson's head and placed the other cheek on the stone, exposing his left eye to the hot iron.

'You will feel this one you pig.'

It was as though the world had stopped and Samson only smiled drunkenly as the guard drove the hot iron into his remaining eye.

****

Asherah had seen enough. Samson's fate was sealed, she could do nothing to stop the chain of events to come, but she could ease his pain.

'That was a lovely gesture.' Moloch floated with his head held thoughtfully in his hand.

'I really do not have the energy to listen to you right now Moloch. Go run an errand for Dagon or something.'

'I do not condone this Asherah.'

'Well you do nothing to stop it, so your inaction does.' Asherah seethed with anger, but she kept it in check.

'Dagon has his own agenda, as do we all.' Moloch spoke softly, without any accusation.

'Yes, and we all make choices about who we align ourselves with. You have chosen one of the fallen.'

Moloch swung the golden symbol around his finger as he considered Asherah's harsh words. 'That is the good thing about choice sister.' He placed the symbol in his pocket and smiled. 'We can choose to change it anytime we want.'

'True, but we cannot undo the damage our choices have already made.'

 **Chapter 38**

The woman moved with grace, yet there was power in her manner that Delilah felt compelled to study. Apparently so did Aviv for his eyes rarely left Katya.

'I am very thankful for your aid Katya, but you really did not need to accompany us to Sorek.' The women rode side by side in the lead with Aviv and Katya's personal bodyguard a few paces behind.

'It was the least I could do for an old friend.' The woman smiled over her shoulder and Aviv nodded in return. 'Besides, I have business to attend to. It has been too long since I checked up on my organisation in Sorek.'

'What exactly is your organisation anyway?' Aviv had shared very little with Delilah. All she understood was that Katya was wealthy, independent and in charge, but of what, she was not sure.'

'I am a business woman, whose business happens to be in opposition to both the temple and the King, from time to time. Sometimes, we are entirely on the same page.'

Delilah considered Katya's words carefully. 'So, are you for or against the Temple when it comes to my family?'

'Let us say that I am with Aviv on this matter. If there are gods or Temple Priests playing at being gods, then I stand to lose a lot of my financial independence. If saving your family, you and ultimately Samson can prevent that, then I would be ill-advised not to pursue helping you.'

'So, you have no moral or ethical compulsion to assist, it is all financial?' Delilah raised a questioning eyebrow.

'Exactly so.'

'Excellent. At least we understand each other.'

Aviv chuckled from behind the women.

'It is not polite or wise to listen in when women are speaking of private matters Aviv.' Katya warned with a flash of iron in her eyes.

Aviv looked to the guard alongside for moral support before he realised that the whispering guard whom he had recently displaced from Katya's favour was unlikely to come to his aid.

'I will check in with Jud when we arrive. Aviv, I suggest you visit Delilah's parents and prepare them for travel. Delilah, you can go with my bodyguard Sahib and pack provisions for your parents.'

Delilah looked behind her and Sahib smiled politely.

'Where are we taking them?' Aviv spoke the question that was on Delilah's lips.

'The Guild has dens in many places Aviv. Gath, Moab. I think Moab would be a good place. There are neither Philistines nor Israelites there. Delilah's parents will be free to continue their blended marriage unhindered by local cultural prejudice.'

'How romantic of you Katya.' Aviv mocked.

'What! I am only human Aviv.' Delilah stifled a giggle as the two continued their friendly banter.

****

Samson knew it was daylight. He could feel the sun beating down on his face but he could see nothing. In his darkness, Delilah's face was there, comforting him.

The cart jostled as it travelled, full of sweating bodies to a destination known only to the driver. Samson sat on the hard seat, squashed between two people. He was unsure where he was heading; to more torture or to his execution but it mattered not. His vision had promised him the ultimate martyrdom and Delilah was safe, her parents were safe, nothing else mattered.

'How the mighty fall.' A man chuckled from Samson's left.

'Shut up Maarku. You would be crying like a baby if someone took your eyes out like that.' The man on his right patted Samson on his back.

'What, you think befriending the big man now will help you where we go Naoki?'

'Not all of us are driven by selfishness Maarku. You should try not to judge everyone by your own standards.'

'That goes both ways my friend.'

Both men fell silent as Samson's thoughts drifted. He awoke to hands dragging him from the cart. His chains were unlocked just long enough for him to be attached to a wooden handle.

'Start pushing big man. There is grain to crush.' The lash of the whip sounded above Samson's head and he frowned in confusion.

'Just start walking Samson. Walk until they tell you to stop.' Naoki encouraged from behind.

Chapter 39

'Delilah's home is surrounded by soldiers.' Jud waited for Katya at the Sorek den which turned out to be the lower level of a tavern right next door to Dagon's temple.

'They are not obvious mind, but they are there. I estimate the numbers started to swell the day you left Gaza Mistress.' Jud poured a pot of ale and took a seat at the long bench that ran the full length of the dimly lit meeting hall.

'How, how could the temple here know we were coming from Gaza?' Katya looked at Jud with confusion, while Aviv and Delilah exchanged knowing glances.

Asherah had stayed behind, claiming she needed to keep an eye on Dagon, but Delilah had an uncontrollable fear that Dagon was no longer in Gaza. He was following her like prey and she resisted the urge to shiver at the thought.

'More to the point, how are we going to get my parents out with all those men around?'

Katya's face showed her frustration. 'A diversion is the best option, something to draw the men away but what?'

Delilah looked at Aviv again who shook his head. Katya caught the subtle movement and waited expectantly, her gaze fixed on Delilah.

'I will draw them away. They are there to keep my parents hostage so they can control me. I am sure they all know who I am. They will follow me like rats to cheese.' Katya smiled and crossed her arms over her chest as though the discussion were over.

'Delilah, Samson would have none of this if he were here. It is too dangerous.'

'Well, Samson is *not* here and the only chance we have of getting him back is for my parents to be out of harm's way. Then Da… the temple will have no power over me.' Aviv made to protest, but Delilah continued on ignoring him.

'Samson is only staying hostage to keep me safe Aviv and you know it. All this nonsense about his hair being the reason he has great strength is a farce.'

'I am not sure that is true Delilah. I share your scepticism but Samson truly believes his vow to grow his hair was the source of his strength.'

'And you think he would not be over such a thought if I were being sacrificed before his eyes? Or attacked?'

'I would not be about to put that to the test, but I get your meaning. Just be careful will you.'

'Aviv, you forget how we met.' Delilah suddenly smiled and Aviv chuckled, relieving the tension between them.

****

Fajer opened the thin curtain at the window and took a deep breath. The temple soldiers were not the only ones watching his home. He had seen the King's men and now there were Guild minions.

'Amariah, pack your belongings. We need to leave.'

'What is going on Fajer?' Amariah joined her husband as he moved from the window trying to trivialise his concern.

'Nothing to worry about. The King or maybe the temple have been watching us and there seems to be a lot of tension about. I simply believe we need to create some distance.'

'Distance? Where are we to go?'

'We can find Delilah.'

'How and with what funds? She has not even sent word since she left. She might be dead. That man you sent her away with has probably raped and killed her by now.' Amariah threw her hands about in disgust.

'Stop being so dramatic Amariah.' Fajer rolled his eyes. 'Samson is a Nazarite and a Judge. Of all the men to send our daughter away with, he was the best option, the safest option.'

Amariah frowned and hung her head in defeat. Fajer was right. They might have found the girl a wealthy husband and he could still have beaten her to death, such was the fate of a young woman of poverty. 'You should have just agreed with Dawsar.'

Fajer was about to share his mind on the topic that his wife failed to understand or put behind her when a noise at the entrance caught his attention. The woman before them was nothing like the half-naked peasant girl who left them behind.

Her hair was braided neatly, her eyes lined with delicate colours that reminded Fajer of sunshine and desert grasses. She wore a gown the colour of crystal clear water and it sparkled with flecks of silver and gold. Amariah's breath caught in her throat as the girl spoke respectfully.

'Mother, father. I wish I could take the time to explain, but I am hunted and I will need to move quickly. As soon as I leave, a woman and the man that accompanied me when I left, Aviv will come for you. You must go with them.'

Fajer made to protest but his daughter cut him off with authority. 'There is no time father, my life and yours depends on it. Leave with Aviv.'

Without another word, Delilah was gone in a whirl of blue silk and dark shining braids.

Fajer rushed to the open doorway that remained without a door and watched his daughter disappear, with a flurry of soldiers in her wake. She moved with the same agility he recalled from her days on the street and he pushed the shock aside to find a sliver of pride.

'Come Amariah, get that bag and let us collect up what we need.'

They barely had time to pack the essentials before Aviv arrived with a strikingly beautiful woman. She had two burly men with her and for a moment Fajer wondered who Delilah had handed them over to, but Aviv assured him there would be time to explain once they arrived where they were going.

Aviv led the older couple out the doorway and down the closest alleyway at a pace that was difficult to maintain.

By the time they reached the lower level of the tavern Amariah's cheeks were flushed red and Fajer had sweat beading on his brow.

Fajer looked around the dimly lit room. 'Where is Delilah?'

'She will be along shortly, I am sure.' Aviv poured a cup of cool water for his guests and watched the door with concern.

****

Delilah opened her eyes to darkness. The smell of incense reached her and she shuddered. She tried to recall her last moments before darkness overtook her but her memory was vague.

'Lovely of you to join us Delilah.' The voice was unmistakeable and Delilah shivered. The Priest carried a torch in his hand and the flame cast eerie shadows as he moved to light the wall sconces. 'We have missed you and my, how you have changed. You look positively lovely.'

'Do not expect me to bow down and make an offer for you today Priest. Those days are gone.' Delilah snarled and the Priest put his hands up in mock horror.

'I would not dream of it my dear. You are chosen for a higher cause.'

Delilah looked around the room with confusion. She had seen every inch of the main temple of Sorek before. Kaamill, when she had thought of him as an Acolyte had given her the grand tour on many an occasion.

This room was different. Small, ornately decorated and dimly lit.

'Where am I?'

'The vestibule child. It is an honour to be granted access.'

Delilah pulled at her bindings. 'Excuse me for not feeling it.'

The Priest raised an eyebrow for a moment and then chuckled to himself. 'I am certain you will lose that flippant tone once Dagon arrives.'

'Dagon does not scare me Priest.'

'He should, he certainly should.' The Priest shuddered.

Chapter 40

'Where is she?' Aviv paced back and forth while Fajer and Amariah spoke quietly to one another from a table in the rear of the tavern. 'I knew I should not have let her be the distraction.'

'She is a brave one Aviv. I can see why you are infatuated.' Katya grinned at Aviv's indignant expression. 'No need to hide it my love. I am not jealous. She is Samson's, is she not?'

'She is not anyone's Katya. No one owns her, she is too free spirited.'

'So this is the attraction.'

'Yes my dear, just as it always was with you.' Aviv moved closer and took Katya gently by the shoulders, his lust rising with her teasing. 'But this is not getting us closer to finding her.' He dropped his grip and moved away with an effort.

'She is in the temple.' Everyone spun round to see Aggie walking into the den.

'How on earth did you get past my guards?' Katya drew a short-bladed sword from a hiding place and Aviv raised an eyebrow.

'Where were you hiding that?'

Katya smiled mischievously, 'It is on a need to know basis and let us say you do not need to know.'

'Aggie, how do you know where Delilah is?' Aviv turned his attention from Katya to Asherah.

'You know her?' Katya questioned, waving her blade recklessly.

'I do Katya. She is Delilah's maid.'

'How is it you know where she is woman?' Katya turned from Aviv to Aggie.

'I simply do. Aviv understands.' Aviv did not really understand but he knew if the goddess said Delilah was in the temple, then she was in the temple.

'We have very little time Aviv. She is in great danger. We must get her out.'

'And how are we going to do that?' Katya queried the maid, hiding her knife back in its secret hiding place as Aviv struggled to see.

'You have the tunnels Katya.' The statement caught the queen of the Guild by surprise. She thought the tunnels were secret and the surprise was evident on her face.

'We do. But I am not sure I have enough men to attack the temple, all for one girl.'

'She is not just any girl.' Fajer had sat quietly, but he had heard enough. 'She is our daughter, a young innocent woman who does not deserve to be sacrificed on the altar of Dagon.'

Katya laughed loudly and Fajer frowned to his wife in confusion, before returning his gaze to the leader of thieves. She continued for a moment before she realised she was the only one finding the statement so amusing.

'You do not need to fear sacrifice old man. Delilah is no virgin and Dagon only takes virgins to his altar.'

Amariah's sharp intake of breath was audible.

'That is enough Katya.' Aviv spoke with a tone to his voice and Katya's laughter almost turned to a growl.

'You are here at my invitation Aviv, you and your *friends*.' Katya swept her hand around the room to make her point. 'Watch yourself.'

'I apologise.' Aviv bowed. 'You are correct of course.'

Asherah had seen enough. Revealing herself was dangerous, but she needed to rescue Delilah before Dagon arrived to take her. Dagon's darkness has grown with his time on earth and she was unsure exactly what he was capable of.

A shimmering light caught everyone's attention. It pulsed with the sound of a soft drum and Aviv stepped back reflexively. The goddess circled her arm around her head, a trail of sparkling stars left her fingers as her greying hair glistened gold and white.

The older woman grew taller, thinner and her plain dress changed colour from dark grey to brilliant purple.

Amariah cried out and ran for the far corner of the room, climbing under the table and hiding like a child who had seen a ghost. Fajer called out to her as the sound grew louder.

A flash of light exploded, forcing everyone still standing to cover their eyes. Aviv smiled as Asherah appeared before them.

'Was all that really necessary?' He spoke quietly so only she and Katya could hear.

'Not entirely, but it had the desired effect.' Asherah grinned at Katya's gaping mouth. 'I think that is the quietest you have ever seen her, am I right?'

Aviv's grin widened as Katya continued to stare.

Fajer coaxed his wife out from under the table, but she took a seat at the bench as far away as she could squeeze herself and refused to make eye contact with the goddess.

'Now Katya, the tunnels, your men and Delilah. Get them ready now. We have very little time left.'

'What do you want me to do?' Aviv ask as Katya remained transfixed.

'Who are you?' Katya spoke softly as she finally found her voice. Aviv smiled at Asherah knowingly.

'I am a friend of Delilah's and I am the only thing standing between her and a lifetime of servitude to Dagon. Now get your men Katya and move them into the tunnels. They attack on my order.'

For the first time since Aviv had met Katya, she truly was speechless.

 **Chapter 41**

Dawsar was droning on and on and Kaamill was growing tired. He could freeze the man on the spot and attend to Delilah in Sorek, but someone might find the King in such a state and that would not be suitable.

The Philistine King was joyfully oblivious to Dagon's involvement in their political landscape and he wished to keep it that way. He had no intention of revealing who he was to the likes of Dawsar.

'You have Samson imprisoned now. What are your plans?' Dagon was curious how the Nazarite would die. 'I know you plan on executing him at the harvest festival, but what makes you sure you *can* kill him?'

'My soldiers put out his eyes, I am fairly certain his mortality is real now and I want everyone to know the Israelites have lost their Judge. Their people need to know that they are under my yoke now.'

'The harvest festival is a few months away, where are you keeping him?'

'He is milling grain, sightless and broken. I only wish my people could see him right now, but they will soon enough. Then they will know I am the greatest King they have ever known.'

Dagon rolled his eyes, unseen by Dawsar. He had no stomach for growing the King's reputation but he wanted his father to suffer. Drawing out the death of the Creator's champion would certainly make a statement amongst his brethren.

Moloch had sentimental reasons for joining this fight. He wanted to keep the eternal realm for the angels, but Dagon simply wanted the earth for himself.

The humans were an eternal source of amusement and ruling them was nothing short of euphoric. Moloch could keep Heaven, Dagon wanted control over the life of every human being and had done since he first tasted the sweetness of the earthly women, the pleasures of the flesh and the power over life and death.

'I must be on my way my Lord. Please excuse my early departure but I have some temple business to attend to. Will you be at the next meeting?'

Dawsar smiled at the thought of another sacrifice. 'Of course Kaamill. I will be in attendance.'

'Very well.' Kaamill bowed reverently. 'I will be in touch to help make the arrangements for the festival.

'I would welcome your assistance.'

Dagon moved from the King's hall and made his way to the courtyard. He drifted past the guards and out the front gates before finding an alleyway to make his departure.

Thoughts of celebrations and past indulgences left him yearning and Delilah's soul beckoned him from Sorek. His anticipation grew as he considered how to bring her to yield. She was in love with the Nazarite, that had become clear in her bid to release her parents so she could be free to rescue him. He needed to break the bond if he was to have her as his queen,

The pocket of air around the dark angel shimmered and burst as he released his wings. The night was cool and he embraced the sky with renewed energy.

Sorek was days away by conventional means, but he had no need of horse or cart. Dagon made no attempt to move with stealth through the night sky. It was enjoyable to hear the speculation of humanity when they saw the likes of the divine.

Talk of vampires and ware-beasts only served to feed their fear and fear was a powerful emotion, one that fuelled the dark angel with intoxicating energy.

Moments later he landed softly on the roof of the temple, the moon shimmering low in the sky. He made his way down the spiralling staircase that led directly to the vestibule behind the altar.

As he entered, he could see the Priest standing over his bride, her hands tied and her face bruised.

'What is the meaning of this?' Dagon almost howled as he moved with lightning speed toward Delilah.

'I am sorry Lord. I needed to bind her to keep her here. She awoke before you arrived.'

Dagon slapped the balding Priest across the face and the man dropped to his knees before the dark god. 'I beg your forgiveness my Lord.'

'Get up and get out of my sight. You have touched her one too many times.' The Priest jumped to his feet and ran with uncharacteristic speed as Dagon stepped forward and touched Delilah's cheek. 'Are you harmed my dear?'

Delilah took a moment to compose herself. Her mind was racing as she remembered being on her knees before the Priest in what seemed so long ago. Now she was faced with Dagon himself and she needed time to think.

'I am fine. Thank you.' Delilah spoke softly, trying to gauge what this monster wanted from her.

Samson was incarcerated now. She had done what Dagon wanted, so was he now hoping to have her for himself? The question must have lingered on her face.

'You look worried my dear. Come, let us become better acquainted. All this talk of marriage must be frightening you. I have not exactly been the best fiancé after all.' Dagon gently untied the leather ropes from her wrists and Delilah rubbed them to get the circulation back. 'Here, let me fix that for you.'

The dark angel took her hands in his and a warm sensation tingled its way up her arms. Her hands stopped hurting and a strange sense of calm filled her mind. She shook her head involuntarily. It felt as though she were on the verge of delirium when realisation struck.

'Please, no magic. You want me to have my wits about me do you not? You seek a queen, not a slave.' Delilah touched Dagon's arm seductively and the angel smiled at her warm flesh.

'You surprise me Delilah.'

'Why is that? You wanted me seduced by the flesh. Well you have your wish.' Delilah licked her lips. 'You have taken Samson from me and my desires only grow stronger. Such needs must be quenched.'

Dagon looked at her questioningly. He reached out with his power to find her motives but her heart was guarded, hardened in a way that gave him no way to gauge her.

'Then why seek to free your parents?'

Delilah stroked the dark angel's cheek as she searched for a feasible answer. Her parents were safe now, of this she was sure. She had known she would be captured. She had planned this moment in her mind but now she was unsure. How far would she be willing to go with Dagon to save Samson?

'Just because I have accepted my place at your side, does not mean I trusted your minions with the lives of my family.' She smiled and stood closer, stroking Dagon's chest and admiring his tattooed arms. The dark angel shuddered at her touch.

He ran his hand down Delilah's face, over her breast and took her by the waist. She did not smell of fear, she smelt of something he could not quite identify but in that moment, he did not care to delve further. She was strong, she might have been deceitful, but she was not afraid and that meant she was willing.

Delilah looked up into the dark angel's eyes and saw swirls of colour appear. The gaze was mesmerizing and her breath grew short and heavy.

Her skin now tingled at his touch and Dagon's eyes smiled at her response.

She had no idea how, but her naked body was pressed against the dark angel's naked chest and she was not afraid. She felt as though she were on fire.

Chapter 42

The Priest took a moment to compose himself as he left the altar room. He had feared Dagon would know his thoughts had drifted to Delilah. The fear threatened to seep into his bones and even now he still shivered.

As he lit more incense and candles for the altar, he noticed a flickering of the flame. It was a still night and the movement puzzled him for a moment before he felt the blade slide across his throat. His eyes grew wide as he grasped at the blade, a sound gurgling but never leaving his lips.

Katya gently lowered the man to the ground and wiped the knife clean on the Priest's robes. She pointed to the rim of light being cast around the door the Priest had just come through.

Aviv and two of Katya's guards were already climbing out of the tunnel while more entered from the tunnel entrance on the other side of the temple.

'There are no tunnels I know of that enter this room. There is only one entrance.' Katya whispered and Aviv nodded his understanding.

Asherah reached the last step up from the tunnel below the temple and wavered. Aviv reached for her hand and the tingle he had felt before ran up his arm and into his chest.

'Are you alright?' Concern spread across his face and Asherah struggled to remain standing.

'I cannot stay long in this place. The death, the spirit of it seeps into me like a cancer. Help me to the doorway. I will distract Dagon. You need to get Delilah out, before it is too late for her.'

Katya frowned at the mention of the temple god's name. Dagon was a myth, a story shared with the children to keep them in line and to young virgins so they would not roam the streets alone for fear of ending up on his altar.

The Guild queen said nothing. She had witnessed Asherah's appearance and more questions than answers remained in her mind, but if Aviv followed the woman, then so would she.

Aviv helped Asherah to the doorway and as she rested her hand on the door frame, he drew his sword. 'Let me lead the way down, you come behind me.'

'He will strike you down the moment he lays eyes on you Aviv. I must go first. I can feel that Delilah is running out of time. I will lure him from this place and my strength will return.'

Asherah walked past the spiral staircase that led to the rooftop and into a short hallway. There were soft sounds drifting on the night air and she could hear Delilah's voice.

As she entered the chamber, she found Dagon with his black wings fully extended and Delilah's naked body beneath him. Her heart ached for the girl. She was too late to prevent the joining, but she would have to deal with that problem at a different time.

'Dagon. Let her go!' Asherah's voice was steady and calm.

The dark angel released his hold on Delilah and she fell to the floor, blood running down her neck and a glazed look to her eyes.

'You are too late Asherah. She gave herself willingly. She is mine now.'

'Aviv, get her out of here.' The merchant had entered moments after Asherah and the sight of his friend enveloped by massive wings, naked and near unconscious left him standing statue still. Asherah's voice woke him from his trance and he moved forward as Dagon and Ashcrah took flight.

They moved through the walls of the temple as though they were a sheer curtain and Aviv stood motionless, watching them disappear before his eyes. A moan from the far side brought him back to reality.

He returned his attention to Delilah as Katya entered the altar room.

'What the? Aviv, is she alive?'

'I think so.' Aviv moved to Delilah. She was pale and the tips of her fingers were grey. Her eyes were glassed over as though she had been smoking opium poppy and she was as weak a new born foal.

'Get up girl.' Katya ordered while she looked over her shoulder for her enemies. 'Where did Asherah go?'

'The goddess chased Dagon from here.'

'But there is nowhere to go, only one entrance.' Katya helped Aviv lift Delilah and they placed an arm each over their shoulders. She was completely naked but there was no time to be concerned with her modesty.

'There is the roof top. The stairs lead up.' Aviv offered, knowing that neither of them had used such a method.

Katya nodded as they passed the stairwell. 'I had no idea they were even there! I will have to speak with my informant.'

As they left the altar room, two of Katya's guards stood watch at the tunnel entrance. 'Your coat, give me your coat.' Katya ordered and Sahib removed his, handing it to his leader without question. 'Drape it over *her*, not me.'

'Where did the blood come from?' He asked as he did the top toggle up so it would stay in place.

'I have no idea but we need to get her back to the den before her kidnapper returns or she bleeds to death!' Aviv ordered and Sahib looked to Katya for confirmation before assisting. He relieved her of the burden and Katya went on ahead, joined by the other guard to ensure they had an unhindered escape.

They rounded the corner to meet face to face with a wall of temple soldiers. They stood at the ready, weapons drawn and faces set. They moved as though they were puppets, being controlled by their master.

****

Asherah felt a surge of power the moment her body left the dark temple. Dagon hovered at the edge of the Veil between worlds and smiled.

'You are truly an abomination Dagon. I thought you had evolved from the flesh-eating monster you became after the fall.'

'Why? I like the taste of blood and I prefer it straight from my willing conquests than fed to me on an altar. Delilah will be my queen. We are one now. She will come to me when you least expect it.'

'Father was right to cast you out. Delilah will be free of you; I will make sure of it!'

'And how will you do that? She will crave me like nothing she has ever wished for.'

'Yes, but she still loves Samson and the bond of love will break your dark magic Dagon.'

'Samson will be dead in a matter of months and Delilah will come back to me willingly. She will be my queen and the baby she carries, the hope of your cause will never see the light of day.'

'You know?' Asherah struggled to keep the concern from her voice.

'Yes, I have known all along that your interest in Delilah and even Samson was not about either of them but their child.'

'You will not harm the child Dagon. I will protect her with my life.'

'Well you had best be prepared to die Asherah.'

Chapter 43

'Aviv. I need your help. Give Delilah to Sahib.'

Aviv handed Delilah over to Katya's personal body guard, who picked her up easily and cradled her with uncharacteristic care. The Merchant hesitated only a moment before drawing his sword.

'On my way now Katya.'

'There are so many of them. Did they know we were coming?' Katya looked from left to right, then over her shoulder. The entire temple from wall to wall was packed with more soldiers than Katya even knew existed.

'It would not surprise me. There are powers at play in all of this that mere mortals like us are never going to understand.'

'When this is over, you have a lot of explaining to do. Asherah, Dagon, what next?' Katya swung her sword with agitation as she waited for the attack they knew was coming.

Aviv, Katya and the remaining guard fanned out to give each other room to move. The first soldier to attack was small and light on his feet. He swung his weapon through the air with little effort.

Katya stepped in to block his blade with her own. She raised her knee into his groin and used her elbow to strike him in the back of the head as his head fell with the pain.

'Just like old times.' Aviv winked to Katya as two more soldiers rushed in with less caution. One was short and heavy set, the other tall and lean. Aviv could not help but notice the vast difference and admired how they managed to work as a team.

'Not quite like old times. We are not running away with a load of jewels or gold this time.' Katya complained but returned Aviv's wink with one of her own.

Two more of Katya's guards came running up from the tunnel. They began fighting to make a path to their leader. The temple soldiers became confused for only a moment, before they divided evenly to fight both fronts.

****

Dagon disappeared with a menacing grin on his face and Asherah felt an uncontrollable anger rising in her soul. The baby was of the royal line and must be protected at all costs but what was she willing to sacrifice to save the child?

The sounds of clashing swords drifted through the Veil and Asherah shook herself to return to the matter at hand. The child would be lost if Delilah was not brought to safety.

There was no time to be discreet. Aviv and Katya were surrounded. Both of them and their guards all showed signs of fatigue. Aviv had a deep cut to his bicep that was spilling blood to the floor while Katya had more than a few shallow gashes to her forearms.

Asherah could only use her powers for a very short time in the temple and even then, her strength was limited. She took a deep breath and drew the air from the temple, creating a vacuum. The candles began to flicker and gutted out one by one.

A wave of darkness rolled out around the building until everyone was blinded by the lack of light. A smoking haze began to fill the temple and the clash of swords stopped in the confusion. Asherah spoke into the minds of Katya and Aviv.

'Bring Delilah and your men to the sound of my voice. I will lead you to the tunnel.'

There was no time for Katya to rationalise the voice in her head. Instead, she grabbed Aviv by the forearm to lead him to safety.

'I heard it too Katya. You lead your men, I will get Delilah.' Aviv whispered but the soldiers closest to them heard the sound of his voice and began flailing their swords around. The guard next to Katya grunted in the darkness and as she leant down to check on him, she felt the blood pooling below his body.

'It is too late for him Katya. Get to safety.' For a brief moment, Katya thought to protest but then considered that anyone who could talk inside her head and transform from an old woman to a beautiful one in such a way, probably knew if her guard were dead or alive.

Sahib's bulking body appeared next to her, Aviv only just behind and Katya released a sigh of relief. She pushed Sahib in front of her and reached for Aviv's hand. Asherah's voice did not sound in her head now. It was more like a hum that grew louder as she got closer to their destination.

They found the tunnel entrance and followed her men back down into the dimly lit corridor. Aviv pulled the door closed behind him and slid the bolt in place.

'I am not sure how long that will hold them.' He jumped down from the ladder and landed deftly on the ground.

The torches in the tunnel sprang to life more brightly and Aviv could see Sahib holding Delilah, still unconscious in his arms. He moved to her as Asherah floated past him as though on a cushion of air.

The goddess touched the tunnel's hidden doorway and the wooden boards became stone before his eyes. She smiled at his expression.

'It is only an illusion, but one that will fool the soldiers above. When they restore light to the temple, it will remain invisible. Now, get Delilah to the tavern quickly.'

Aviv turned to Sahib. 'You heard the lady.' Sahib did not argue, instead, he readjusted his grip on Delilah and moved quickly to the end of the tunnel that led up a set of narrow stone stairs to the tavern.

'What happened to her?' Aviv asked aloud as Sahib placed Delilah on top of the wooden table and Asherah moved in to examine her.

'It is too complex to explain.' Fajer and Amariah ran at the sight of their daughter, blood running down her almost naked body.

'Try and explain. Please. What has happened to our daughter?' Fajer touched Delilah's forehead and the girl moaned. 'Delilah, it is papa, you are safe baby.' Fajer looked up at the goddess. 'She is safe now, yes?'

Asherah hesitated a moment and then nodded. 'She is safe Fajer. She will live, but she is bound to Dagon now. I am not sure there is much I can do to break the bond.'

'What do you mean bound to him?' Aviv interrupted.

'It is difficult to explain here Aviv. These are matters I am not permitted to explain to mortals.'

'There is that word again.' Katya looked in no mood to be kept in the dark and she was a woman unaccustomed to such restraints. 'You need to explain all this, this, I do not know what this is. Magic, sorcery, whatever it is. Explain!'

'Child, you are a big fish in your pond, but I do not live in your pond. You have no authority over me.' Asherah spoke softly but there was no mistaking the tone in her voice.

'What Katya is trying to ask politely,' Aviv gave his companion a stern look which she returned, 'is that we are a little nervous of all that is going on. You know us mere mortals have limitations in understanding. Surely you can be a little more forthcoming Asherah?' Aviv tried to smooth the ruffled feathers of these exquisite creatures, but it was not easy.

'Asherah, Dagon. These are names of legend, of myth.' Amariah found the courage to speak at last, her eyes never leaving Delilah's still form. 'You are speaking blasphemy. You have put my daughter in danger with your actions against Yahweh.'

'No Amariah, we are not speaking blasphemy, we speak the truth. Yahweh knows who we are. He does not deny our existence, he merely warns the Israelites not to follow us. You can choose to not follow me if you so wish, but Delilah has made her own choice and now Dagon has chosen her. You are mixed up in this even if you do not believe in me.'

'You are a demon!'

'You are ignorant of exactly who I am Amariah and please keep your uneducated opinions to yourself. You left your people to marry a Philistine. I hardly think that puts you in any position to judge me.'

'Maybe you should explain more Asherah. Educate us.' Katya challenged and Asherah sighed.

'There are matters I am not at liberty to share. You are not even supposed to know I exist unless you are a Priestess of my order. And Dagon, that is another story altogether. He has his own minions on earth and his rules of revealing himself are his own. He is no longer bound by the laws of the Creator.'

'Enough. All I want to know is how we save Delilah now before she bleeds to death and then how can we break this bond Dagon now holds over her!' Aviv had lost patience with debates about gods and deities.

'While Samson lives, the union will not be complete. Delilah's love for him holds her to this realm, but if Samson dies, the only way to save Delilah will be for Dagon to die.'

'Then Dagon must die.' Aviv snarled the words.

'If only it were that easy.' Asherah sighed and sadness filled her spirit.

Chapter 44

'Beautiful Delilah. You are mine now.' Dagon licked the blood from her neck and Delilah giggled with the pleasure.

The memory faded with her dreams as the image of Samson filled her conscious mind and the young woman awoke. The room was dark and quiet.

'Good to find you awake at last.' Aviv touched her hand. 'How are you feeling? Sorry, I know, stupid question.'

Delilah smiled as Aviv lit a small candle on her bedside stand. 'Not so silly. I am tired, very tired.'

'I am not surprised. Dagon sucked your blood low enough to almost kill you.'

'Sucked my blood? I thought that was a dream.'

'What do you remember?'

'I remember waking up in the vestibule of the temple. No idea how I got there.' Delilah stopped as her voice grew croaky.

Aviv handed her a cup of water and helped her lift her head to take a sip.

'I was bound in leather straps by the Priest and then Dagon arrived.' Delilah continued. 'I really do not recall much after that.' Delilah lied.

She remembered everything, including her naive belief that she could save Samson by seducing Dagon. She recalled the ecstasy, the feelings of euphoria as Dagon bit into her neck.

She had thought to strike a bargain with the dark angel, to free Samson in exchange for her willingness to be his queen, but now she understood the fragility of her power.

'We do not understand everything. Asherah is being guarded with her explanations, much to Katya's disgust.' Aviv grinned and Delilah released a little tension with a chuckle at the thought of the two women faced off against one another.

'Your mother is waiting to see you. I will get her for you.'

'No. Not yet.' Delilah placed her hand on Aviv's arm to stop him rising from her bedside. 'How is Samson?'

'I have not seen him Delilah. They moved him to the mill to work. I have heard terrible things but nothing I can confirm.'

'You must visit him for me. Tell him I carry his child.' Aviv took a deep breath.

'How can you know this already?'

'Dagon told me. That I do remember. He told me that the child must die and that he would birth his own children with me, demi-gods to do his bidding. I want Samson to know he has more than me to fight for now and that he must escape.'

'I will visit him as soon as Katya can arrange it.'

****

Samson accepted the drink of water Naoki handed him. He took the cup away when the big man had finished and passed him a piece of flat bread and dried fruit.

'There is talk Nazarite of your execution.'

'It was only a matter of time.' Samson chewed the food automatically.

'There is someone here to see you.' Naoki patted him on the back as Aviv moved closer.

He looked at his friend, blind and broken, sitting on a bench seat as though awaiting a death he knew was coming.

'Samson. It is me, Aviv.' Samson looked up instinctively before recalling he could see nothing.

'My friend. How is Delilah?' He smiled at the thought of her, safe now and free of her commitment to see him dead.

'I come all this way and you ask after a woman? How predictable!' Aviv chuckled and sat down next to his friend. Getting into the prison had not been so difficult. He was dressed as a guard, taking the place of Katya's man for the afternoon shift.

'How did you manage to get in here? Samson spoke softly but despite his obvious strength, he seemed broken with his blindness. Aviv studied his old friend, the cloth wrapped around his head to cover the damage to his vision.

'It has taken time. They changed your schedule often at first and we were confused about how we were going to get close to you, but eventually they forgot about you my friend.'

'Apparently not entirely. There is talk of my execution.'

'Yes, everyone has heard. You need to escape before the festival.'

'No, I need to attend the festival.'

Aviv sighed. He had hoped to break the news more gently, but Samson's stupor worried him.

'Delilah is with child, your child Samson. You must survive for them both, not die for them.'

Samson smiled despite his pain. 'With child you say? She will have something to remember me then.'

'She does not want something to remember you by Samson, she needs you, more than you could ever know.' Aviv almost begged. He had hoped to not tell Samson of Dagon's curse but the man was resigned to die a martyr.

'It is hard to explain Aviv, but I am here for a reason. I have a task set before me and I must be at the temple of Dagon to fulfil that destiny.'

'Your imprisonment has sent you mad. You are stronger than any man alive Samson, simply fight your way out of here and return to Delilah.'

'I broke my vow Aviv. My power is gone.'

'I know you cannot see Samson, but you must have realised your hair has grown back. Even if your power was given to you because of your vow, you have renewed it, it is full length once more.'

As if to confirm, Samson touched his long matted locks, that hung over his rippling shoulders. Aviv was correct, his hair had grown back.

'It matters not, the strength is not mine, it is Yahweh's and he has shown me what I need to use it for—not for killing Philistines in revenge, but for taking down the one who lures the Philistines away from their true creator.'

Aviv was stunned. 'Samson, your beautiful Delilah awaits and Dagon seeks to have her for his own. You must escape and protect her. He has bound her to him. She will be his queen only if you die.'

'Not if he dies with me. I will protect her Aviv. Believe me. You will see. Watch over Delilah. Take her and the child to safety. When I am done, you will understand.'

Aviv knew when there was no changing Samson's mind. The man had made his choice and no one on earth could persuade him otherwise. Instead, he chose to spend his last few minutes reminiscing with his friend on brighter memories.

As he left the dark and moist walls of the prison behind him, he felt as though he were leaving a piece of himself behind. Samson and he had known each other since they were young men and although there were parts of their lives they had never shared, they had been joined at the hip for many, many years.

Chapter 45

Delilah stood with her hand resting on her small, rounded belly. Amariah wiped the tears from her eyes with the back of her hand and kissed her daughter on the cheek.

'You should come with us Delilah.'

'No, I will stay for Samson. I will follow soon. I promise.'

'I will make sure she is safe.' Aviv vowed as he saw Fajer and Amariah looking expectantly in his direction.

'Come woman, let us leave before you both end up in tears.' Delilah's eyes were glistening but she was finding emotion difficult to capture of late. Her dreams were troubled and the dark circles around her eyes told a story she tried to keep hidden.

'Katya has made the arrangements. Just ask for Tariq when you arrive. He will find you work and keep you safe in the lands of the Moabites.'

'Honest work?' Fajer insisted with a smile.

'Yes, honest work. Even amongst the Guild there are tavern owners and shop keepers.' Katya patted the old man on the shoulder as she reassured him.

'Very well then. Come Amariah, time to go.' He helped his wife up into the small cart. He checked the yoke was fastened securely around the ox's neck and then joined his wife before cracking a small whip to get the beast moving.

'Stay safe Delilah.' He called back over his shoulder as they began to move away.

Delilah watched her mother and father leave and struggled to find the feelings she knew were buried inside of her. Instead she felt numbness, a sense of loneliness she could not entirely understand let alone explain.

'How are you feeling Delilah?' Aviv asked as he gently took her arm to escort her from the estate gates to the courtyard.

'Sad.'

Aviv looked at Delilah. Her face showed her tiredness and her eyes had lost their sparkle.

'Samson is going to be executed and it is all my fault.'

'That is untrue Delilah. Samson has been the target of Philistine vengeance for decades. He has killed so many of them that I am surprised it took them this long to find a way to punish him.'

'Yes Aviv, but *I* gave them a way. If not for his love for me, he would never have given himself up. If not for me, he would have fought his way free by now.'

'Delilah, there is more to this I have not shared with you. Come, take a seat, I should explain.'

Aviv guided Delilah through the courtyard toward the soft faded green divan that sat on the veranda. She stared at the walls covered in climbing greenery and took a deep breath. The scent was luxurious and she smiled as she thought of her time with Samson in this beautiful place—a time when cares were lessened and they enjoyed a short respite.

'Samson told me he had seen a vision, one that he did not explain fully but requires him to be at the temple of Dagon at the harvest feast.'

'So you are saying he stays not because of me, but because he believes in this vision?'

'Exactly. He told me to get you to safety. To keep you from Dagon.'

'Dagon haunts my dreams Aviv. It is as though he knows Samson is the only thing keeping me from him.'

'Have you told Asherah of your dreams?'

'They are only dreams Aviv.'

'I am not so sure they are.'

'I knew I would find you here.' Katya strolled into the courtyard and smiled. 'Delilah, you are looking better. Aviv, may I tear you away a moment?'

Aviv looked to Delilah who nodded and then back to Katya whose expression was difficult to read.

'Yes, of course.' Aviv bowed respectfully as he left Delilah and took Katya's arm.

The pair walked away, down the hall and out into the meeting room. The long tables were lined with Katya's men and guards from the estate.

'The training is going well. We have enough men to attack the temple on your orders.' Katya indicated the collective soldiers with her open palm.

'You called me away from Delilah to parade the men I have been helping you train?' Aviv grinned and Katya's expression grew guarded.

'I needed to distract you. That girl has enough unwarranted attention already.'

'Are you jealous?' Aviv stepped closer and Katya took a step back.

'Of course I am not jealous! What kind of question is that!' Aviv kissed her before she could speak another word and hoots and whistles exploded from the men assembled.

Katya pushed him away and turned on her heel to leave the dining area, but Aviv grabbed her hand and pulled her back into his chest, her face away from him, his face buried in her long hair.

Katya dropped to her knees and pulled the unsuspecting merchant over her head and onto his back but instead of landing heavily, Aviv landed on his feet, springing upward as Katya let go.

More laughter and hooting exploded from the men as they pulled benches and tables back to watch the display. A few coins rolled onto tables as men from both camps bet on who the victor might be.

The combatants exchanged knowing looks and Aviv winked at Katya who shrugged in return. Katya ran forward and slid on her back at the last moment. Aviv knew the move well and dropped to his knee, rolling aside to allow Katya to slide by. She rolled effortlessly onto her feet once more and the two circled each other.

'You have learnt a few new tricks Aviv.'

'Yes, true. There was a time when you had taught me all I know, but that time was a while ago now.'

'So you have something new to teach me then.' Katya's eyes sparkled with the challenge.

'Yes of course, but I think it is better demonstrated in private.'

Katya blushed slightly as she understood the innuendo. 'Well you will have to beat me here before you can get me alone.'

'Damn, that could prove too difficult. Will you settle for a draw?' Aviv moved forward, his head tucked low as he lifted Katya from her feet. She was smaller than him, but agile and she braced her arms on his buttocks, pushed her knees off his chest and did a complete back flip landing on her feet behind him.

The men cheered again and Aviv smiled at their pleasure. 'She wants me really. This is just a front she is putting up for your benefit.' He spoke to no one in particular but Sahib seemed to think the comment was aimed at him.

The personal bodyguard moved forward. He was at least a head taller than Aviv and his arms rippled with power. Aviv was no small warrior, in fact if he had not been friends with Samson for so long, he would have thought himself invincible, but Sahib was formidable.

'That is enough. Sahib, stand down. This is only a little play-fight, nothing to get all heated up over.' Katya stepped between the two men and placed a hand on Sahib's chest.

'He makes jests about your virtue.' Sahib was genuinely upset.

'Oh Sahib. I am sorry if all this has hurt you, but Aviv is special to me, not that you are not, but Aviv is, well, he just is.' Katya turned and grabbed Aviv by both cheeks. She smothered his mouth with hers and all the men howled like wild dogs. Aviv took a moment to come up for air before lifting her off her feet and taking her from the dining hall.

Chapter 46

Delilah had heard all the noise in the dining room and had walked in to see the tail end of the entertainment. She smiled as the two left their men for privacy. She liked Katya. She was strong and sure of herself and Aviv was her perfect match. She wondered about their history not for the first time and decided it was a story she probably did not need to know.

She returned to the sunshine and her divan, the need for sleep taking her like a vicious illness. She slipped into dreams almost immediately and her vision swam.

There was a sensation of weightlessness as she watched herself leave the courtyard. Such visions were commonplace of late and she observed her sleeping body below, wondering again why she had not told Asherah about her strange nightmares.

'Delilah, soon you will be with me.' Dagon opened his wings, his tattooed chest rippling with power.

'I do not want that Dagon. You know this to be true.' Delilah's voice was soft and tired. This was a conversation she had shared with the dark angel more times than she could remember recently.

'Yes you do. You remember that night. The pleasure, the power!' Dagon moved toward her, his body floating in the strange place between reality and dream without effort.

'I hardly recall it at all.' Delilah lied as the tingling began in her stomach and the sensations she had tried to block out returned. Her legs felt like jelly and her heart raced.

'Come now, let me remind you.' Dagon took her around the waist and licked her neck.

'No. Please. Leave me be. I want Samson, not you.' Delilah pushed the dark angel away and he almost growled as he released her.

'Soon your Nazarite will be dead. He is to be executed you know.'

'Of course I know. Dawsar has sent word far and wide. If he believes we will stand by and let that happen, he is very mistaken.'

Dagon laughed, a sound that sent shivers down Delilah's spine. 'You think your pitiful army will stop me? I am of the fallen Delilah. I have lived for thousands of years and I have seen the rise and fall of humanity. There is nothing you can do to stop me.'

'I wish to return Dagon. Let me go.' It had not taken Delilah long to understand that she still held some power in this relationship. For whatever reason—and Delilah was sure it was likely Samson—Dagon could not fully compel her obedience or was it her obedience that compelled her?

'As you wish my queen.' Dagon bowed sarcastically and flipped his hand as though she were a worrisome fly.

Delilah gasped as she awoke to darkness. Lanterns had been lit and food was on the table by the divan. She sat up and pulled the tray closer, selecting a few items but struggling to find the appetite to consume them.

'You must eat Delilah, your child needs nourishment.' Asherah appeared from the shadows with an aura of golden light surrounding her.

'Where have you been?'

'Gathering allies.'

'From where?'

'From wherever I can. You must leave this place soon. Your child is very important you know.'

'Why?' Delilah sighed. They had shared this conversation already and Asherah still had not explained anything yet.

'It is complicated.' Asherah sat down and handed Delilah a cup of cool water.

'I will starve myself to death if you do not tell me what is really going on Asherah. I am so sick and tired of everyone treating me like fine porcelain. Aviv tells me only a little of his last visit with Samson and only when he must.

Katya skirts around me with the plans they have made to rescue Samson from execution and you tell me my child is important but refuse to explain why. I am done, finished. If you will not give me the courtesy of the truth, then I will die with Samson.'

'Tell her Asherah.' A tall woman dressed in armour appeared before them. She had rippling muscles in her arms and back and her eyes were so dark, they felt like a night sky that was ready to swallow her up.

'Anath. We are not supposed to. There are rules.'

'Yes and you break them all the time when it suits you. Meddling is against the rules. Revealing yourself, also against the rules.' Anath floated toward the pair and took a seat alongside Delilah who moved a little further down the divan defensively.

'Delilah, meet my sister Anath, another goddess or angel if you prefer.'

Delilah was speechless as her mind raced with thoughts. 'How many of you are there?'

'I honestly have never taken count.' Anath laughed at the thought. 'There are the chosen, the fallen and the others. I would say if you count us all, thousands.'

'Anath!' Asherah scolded.

'Astarte and I have spoken about this at length sister. The child is important. Delilah has a right to know what she is giving up.'

'Giving up?' Delilah touched her belly reflexively.

'Oh for Father's sake, I have not even broached the subject yet.'

'I know and you never will if you do not first start with the truth.'

Delilah stormed to her feet and put her hands on her hips. She began to pace the courtyard like a caged animal, her energy fuelled by her frustration.

'I am right here you know and I have had just about enough of all this. You are all treating me like a child. I am an adult. I will be a mother soon and you all talk to me as if I am simple. What on earth is happening?'

Asherah frowned at her sister. 'Delilah, please sit back down. I am sorry. I will try to explain as much as I can.'

Delilah sat down and Anath patted her gently on the leg. The sensation was subtle but the feeling of peace travelled quickly, stopping the agitated kicks that the baby had begun moments before. Delilah rubbed at the foot that now sat still, protruding from her belly like a hard rock.

'You do that so nicely for a goddess of war you know.' Asherah smiled as Anath nodded her reply.

Delilah shook her head in confusion and instead of asking, simply looked to Asherah and waited.

'Your child is yours and Samson's this is true. Her birth has been foretold. From her line, your line, comes a very important figure who will bring peace to earth and the heavens.'

'Is Heaven not at peace?'

'No Delilah, Heaven is at war and Dagon is one of our enemies.'

'You digress sister.'

'Yes, I do Anath. Thank you. Delilah, your child is more than simply your and Samson's daughter. I had no idea. I did not see this coming, but your connection with Dagon—what he did to you, well, that has strengthened your child beyond anything we could ever have hoped for.'

'Does Dagon know this?'

'I do not believe so.'

'He wants this baby dead, so he must know she is of the line you speak.'

'That he does know, but he has no idea he has passed on his strength to her.'

'So, how do we keep her safe from Dagon?'

'Dagon must die but this is the hard part Delilah. I believe Samson already knows this. These plans were made before you were all born. They began before the fallen even fell. The only problem is I have never seen a mortal kill an angel. We must trust in the Creator's plans.'

'Who are the fallen?' Delilah reached for a handful of dried fruit and began to eat as her mind digested everything she was hearing.

'A group of angels who defied the Creator, who mixed their seed with humanity and taught them of magic. They shared too much, which is why I am not supposed to be telling you any of this, but Anath is right, this is important.'

'You said we had to trust the Creator and that I had to understand what I was giving up, but you were not talking about Samson were you?' Delilah patted her belly with affection and the child stretched in reply.

'No Delilah, not only Samson. I am so sorry to ask this of you. You deserve so much more.'

Chapter 47

The streets were lined with thousands of people as the cart made its way from the mill to the temple. The sound of jeering and malice drifted on the breeze.

Samson attempted to wipe the rotten fruit and eggs from his face, until he reached the end of his chains which were firmly fixed to the bars on the cart. The Nazarite took a deep breath and ignored the attacks as he dwelled on his destiny.

His vision had revealed that he would die in the temple but when Aviv came to him one last time and explained that Dagon now held Delilah prisoner in some way, his mind was set. Dagon would be in the temple for his execution, of this he was sure, but how does a blind man kill a god?

Samson had believed Dagon to be nothing more than myth, folklore told to the Philistines to keep them offering blood and gold to the temple priests but when Aviv explained Asherah and Dagon and all he had seen, the Nazarite had been angry at his own ignorance.

How could he be so stupid to believe in Yahweh and think that his God was the only deity to want this world? Aviv did not fully understand and neither did Samson, but he understood he had been given a chance to not only destroy Dagon, but save Delilah and their child.

To leave the legacy of ending Dagon and giving life to a child was something Samson had never truly hoped to do. As a Nazarite, he had lived only to serve but when he had cut his hair to save Delilah, he had broken his promise to his God. Now Yahweh had forgiven him, he understood that now and as he touched the hair that hung from his head, he understood the blessing of that forgiveness.

'What are you smiling about Nazarite? You have condemned us all to death with your zealot ways.'

'Shut up Maarku. Even with what little time you have left you are still an ass. Maybe it is time to make peace with your maker and stop blaming everyone else for your misfortune.'

The prisoner spat on the ground. 'A pox on the gods. You are as blind as he is Naoki.' The prisoner pointed with his thumb at Samson who sat quietly listening to the two men. 'We are going to the temple of Dagon, a god these idiots worship and he is not giving me one ounce of peace.'

'Samson is not to blame for our sentence. It is Dagon and his temple priests who decided our days are done.' Naoki pointed his finger at his friend's chest.

'The gods are myth Naoki, every last one of them. I will not leave my destiny to a fantasy.'

'What are you planning on doing?' Naoki hushed his words and moved closer.

'As soon as they try to untie me from these bars, I am making a run for it. Better to die trying than sit by and wait for death.' Naoki nodded his understanding.

'I have a better idea.' Both men looked at Samson, Naoki raised an eyebrow and Maarku scoffed.

'What idea? I am not taking advice from a blind man.'

'You said you do not believe in the gods. Have you never heard the stories of my strength?'

'I have heard them but they were tales it seems. You have endured months of servitude to your Philistine masters and never once tried to escape.' Samson ignored Maarku's mocking tone and Naoki frowned at his companion irritably.

'Samson's strength is not myth Maarku. I have seen it myself.'

'When?' Maarku challenged.

'When I was younger. I saw him kill men with his bare hands.' Maarku scoffed again and ducked as another piece of rotten fruit narrowly missed his head.

'Naoki. I will need your eyes.'

'What can you do Samson?'

'I feel my strength returning. I will end Dagon and his temple. I will break the Philistine's pride when their god is gone from this earth.'

'You are a Nazarite. I thought there was only one god.' Maarku teased.

'There is only one almighty god Maarku and I am about to prove it.'

'Tell me what to do.' Naoki slid up alongside Samson and listened to the plan. Maarku frowned and strained to listen, but he could hear very little.

'Do not help him Naoki. You may yet be able to plead for your life.'

'I have no interest in pleading for anything Maarku. Better to die with pride and honour than bow down to my oppressors.'

'Grand and delusional rubbish. I will not help you. I will run the first chance I get.'

'I offer your freedom Maarku. Trust me. Trust my God. Stay the course. Naoki will help me and I will bring down the temple. You will be free again.'

Maarku took a deep breath. Naoki found it hard to read the man. They had been cell mates for years now, moving from one working prison to the next.

Both men were small but strong and as labouring slaves, they were fed well, not well enough to create mischief but enough to keep them working hard.

'Do not count on me Samson.' Maarku offered honestly.

'We would not dream of it. That is why Samson did not tell you the plan.'

'You are a bastard Naoki. You play at begin Mister Nice, but on the inside, you really are as much of an ass as I am.

Both men laughed and were greeted with a crack against the bars of the cart. 'No idea what you are so happy about. Shut your traps. It will be me and my men laughing by end of day.'

Chapter 48

Delilah rubbed her belly as she watched the cart pull up to the outside of the temple courtyard. The stone stairs were shining brightly in the late afternoon sun, belying the darkness that resided within.

Her baby pushed and stretched her feet and Delilah traced the heel with her fingertips. 'Not long now little one. Soon you will see this nasty world and I hope it treats you better than it treated me and your father.'

'Your life is not over Delilah.' Asherah appeared behind the young woman and touched her on the shoulder.

'It feels like it is Asherah.'

'You are young and have so many more years ahead. You will see. I have a place for you that will take your breath away. I promise.'

'Are you sure this is wise?'

'Wisdom was never my strongest talent but I am sure what we do is blessed Delilah.'

'How can you be sure? Samson is only a man. How can he end Dagon?'

'With the help of Yahweh, anything is possible.'

'That is assuming we have His blessing.'

Asherah shrugged. It was an unwinnable argument. 'We can only do what we believe is right Delilah. The rest is truly up to destiny, to fate, to Yahweh.'

'I want to be in control of my own destiny Asherah.'

'Control is an illusion child, something humans tell themselves they possess, in order to allay their fears. Fear is the real enemy. Do not fear your future.'

Delilah drew the arrow from the quiver at her back and prepared to take aim. 'Anyone who tries to hurt him will die.'

'Be careful Delilah. Once you fire, you position will be known.'

Delilah nodded her understanding and Asherah shimmered out of view.

****

Kaamill smiled as the prisoners were herded into the temple auditorium. The moon was rising into the sky as the sun dipped below the temple wall. The large orange moon marked the beginning of the harvest season and its glow filled him with a sense of power and pleasure.

Samson entered, flanked by two smaller, yet equally as muscular slaves. His eyes were bandaged, covering the scars of blindness.

Dawsar smiled and stood to open the ceremony. The crowd responded with a cheer that echoed throughout the open aired stadium. The people began to chant the King's name and he lifted his hands, soaking up their adoration. Tonight, he would kill the champion of Israel. Tonight, he would become a giant amongst kings.

More peasants filed into the stadium, all trying to gain a seat with a view of the pyre that took centre stage next to the king.

'Samson, the stadium is packed to capacity. It seems you are more popular in death than in life.' Naoki smiled, unseen by his friend.

'I have to get out of here Naoki.' Maarku pulled at his bindings, a look of terror spreading across his features.

'Wait. Please stay calm.' Naoki begged.

'This is my only chance before they shackle my feet again.'

Samson reached to touch his arm offering reassurance as the gates thumped closed behind them.

The Nazarite did not reach their friend, instead Maarku moved with speed boosted by his rising adrenalin.

The crowd hooted and cheered as the prisoner jumped over the railing and into the crowded stands. Maarku dodged an arrow that struck a bystander nearby and within a heartbeat peasants parted like a wave, creating as much space between them and the prisoner as quickly as they possibly could.

Maarku watched his cover disappear. Parents threw children aside as they lunged away from him. He ducked behind an old man, who took an arrow in the chest. More people ducked and moved as far from the running man as they could and Maarku suddenly realised his mistake.

The arrow hit him in the shoulder but the crowd screamed for his blood. Another bolt took him the chest. He spun round, realising he was so close to the top of the stadium, so close to freedom. Another arrow hit him in the neck and he backed away from the onslaught, the air escaping his lungs and his energy seeping away with every laboured breath.

The wall was so close now. Just a few more steps and he would find his escape. Maarku rolled to the edge of the stadium as another arrow hit him in the leg. The pain was leaving him and the cool stone felt warm beneath his hands.

Just one more step and he would know freedom. Maarku dragged himself over the wall as another arrow took him in the back of the neck. The crowd exploded with applause as Maarku's body disappeared from sight.

Bystanders ran to the wall to peer over, laughing and pointing at the broken body on the cobble stones below.

Temple soldiers jogged out with stretchers to collect the wounded peasants and the King began to speak, his voice booming over the clapping, drawing everyone's attention back to their monarch.

'It is a grand day for our people, a day that will see the end of the last Israelite Judge, the Nazarite who killed thousands of our people; soldiers who were simply serving their king and country. Samson, do you have a last request?'

Samson smiled. He had known the King would not have been able to resist the temptation to offer him a chance to beg for mercy, for his life or for his people.

Naoki had pointed out the weakest point of the stadium, the moment they had entered. Now, all he needed to do was to be given the chance to bring the temple down.

'Please Dawsar, might I be given the chance to rest somewhere before you commence the ceremony? Perhaps the pillars near the pyre?'

The King was taken aback. How did the Nazarite see with his blindness? There was a hush amongst the crowd. Not even a baby's cry or muffled conversation broke into the silence. Dawsar frowned and looked to Kaamill for guidance.

Kaamill shrugged his response and the King nodded his agreement, before realising Samson could not see. He stifled a laugh and pointed to the pillars.

'Make sure you tie him tightly mind.' He warned the guards who took the Nazarite, still fully shackled to the pillars.

One guard carefully separated his leg shackles and reattached them nervously to the pillars. The second guard did the same with his arms but took the opportunity to elbow the Nazarite in the stomach. Samson grunted but smiled at the man when he heard the thud of an arrow hit the man in the chest. The noise was known to the Nazarite and unmistakable.

'That's my girl.'

The first guard looked to see where the arrow had come from and saw the glinting metal point too late.

Chapter 49

'How many of these tunnels do you have?' Aviv pulled his dagger from the sheath and checked the blade. Satisfied, he returned it and adjusted his sword scabbard absentmindedly.

'That is a secret you will have to work out of me later.' Katya grinned and Aviv felt the heat reach his groin.

'I will take you up on that offer when we get back to your bedchamber.'

Katya moved forward and wrapped her arm around Aviv's neck, grabbing him by the hair and pulling him to her. 'You are not getting away from me this time.' She bit his lip and he responded by smothering her lips with his.

He took a deep breath as their lips parted but kept his forehead touching hers. 'I should never have left Katya. I only hope you can forgive me.'

'I will let you work on that. It will take time, but enough grovelling can achieve anything.' She licked his nose and smiled provocatively as she pulled away. 'I am sure you can come up with suitable ways to work your way back into my favour.'

'It is time.' Sahib patted them both on the shoulder. 'If you can stop exchanging saliva long enough of course.'

'Jealous!' Aviv smiled and Sahib thumped him in the arm. 'Ouch, that was hard.'

'It was supposed to be. I want you to have something to remember me by just in case.' He left the details unsaid.

'Do not even think it my friend. I have your back.'

'I might not have yours you know. You stole my woman.'

'She was mine first.' Aviv puffed up his chest good naturedly.

Katya had to reach up to slap Sahib, but Aviv was not so much of a challenge. 'I belong to no one. You both know better.'

'Of course we do. This has nothing to do with you. Really!' Aviv protested as Katya raised an eyebrow. 'It is a man thing. Just let us have a moment.'

Katya rolled her eyes and drew her sword. 'Have your moment later.'

Both men looked at each other and shrugged, following her lead and drawing their weapons.

'Time to rescue Samson.' Aviv raised his sword in salute and followed Katya as she pushed open the grate leading from the tunnel into the cobbled stone alley.

The crowd was forcing its way out of the stadium in a panic as Delilah and Katya's archers rained arrows down on them. A group of temple soldiers had flung the gates open in the hopes of slowing the stampede but people were falling in the throng, screaming as they were trampled under the feet of their countryman.

Aviv shivered at the haunting cries and hoped that Asherah and her sisters acted soon, before too many innocent lives were lost in this endeavour.

****

Samson could hear the commotion and he knew his time would be running short but he wanted to allow as many bystanders as possible to escape before he made his move.

'You are all clear.' He heard Naoki's voice whispering in his ear as the King screamed orders to any guard who would listen.

'Alright, now get out of here my friend, while you still can.' Naoki did not wait, he knew what was to follow and as much as it saddened him, he understood Samson's motives.

Samson braced himself, pulling the chains taut as he took a deep breath. The columns began to move slightly and the shriek of Dawsar's voice was now a shrill sound in the distance.

He did not feel the first arrow, nor the second. All he could feel was the force of power pulsing through his strong arms as sweat dripped from his body. His tunic was torn from months of harsh treatment and his torso rippled with every working muscle.

His strength was back and Samson knew the power of Yahweh pulsed in his veins. He would redeem himself and save Delilah from the darkness.

****

Delilah saw the first arrow strike and her heart leapt to her throat. She scanned the podium, the battlements and the tower until she found the archer. Her arrow struck him in the eye as he drew to take another shot.

Another arrow hit its mark and Delilah struggled to find her target as the tears began to roll from her eyes and down her cheeks.

'Oh Samson. Please hurry, please!'

She found the second archer above the King's throne and took him in the heart. The King ducked for cover and fled the stadium, finally ceasing to scream his panicked orders.

Kaamill sat beside the King's throne, calmly studying his fingernails. Delilah wiped the tears from her eyes as rage filled her chest. Her fingers tingled as she drew back on the shaft and took aim.

She watched the dark angel's eyes scan Samson with puzzlement and finally realisation struck a chord. He frowned slightly as the temple began to rumble, but remained in his seat.

Delilah took a breath, ready to lose the shaft, her aim fixed on the man she knew to be Dagon in disguise. As the shaft left the bow, the dark angel turned his eyes to look directly at Delilah, as though he were only a mere step away from her.

Her stomach churned as he caught the shaft and smiled in her direction. She had to move. Quickly! As she rose to leave the roof top she saw soldiers fanning out around her like flames. They wore the robes of the temple and her heart sank.

Dagon had known she was there all along. He had stayed to tempt her and now it was going to be too late. She and her child of destiny were going to die while Samson tore down the temple below and died in vain.

Clouds of dust began to rise as enormous chunks of stone fell. Delilah risked a glance, just one more glimpse of Samson. As she looked, the entire temple—the podium—the monuments—the altar room—the intricately carved wall fell. Delilah saw Samson go under the rubble and dropped to her knees on the hard stone ground.

Do not give in Delilah!

Chapter 50

Aviv watched with horror as the temple began to crumble. 'We have to get to Samson.'

A slave ran past Aviv and stopped as he saw him. 'Samson said to go, to protect Delilah at all costs. Do you know where she is now?'

'Who are you?' Aviv challenged and the slave grabbed him gently by the arm.

'Your friend said to go. He has no intention of leaving this place alive. He wants the demon dead and his temple finished.'

'No, I am going after him.' Aviv pulled his arm free.

'My name is Naoki, Samson's friend in prison. He said you would be stubborn.'

The walls began to shake and stones fell, blocking their exit. Dust filled the alleyway and more debris began to shower from above.

'Damn him!' Aviv growled as Katya pointed to where Delilah had been hiding. Soldiers could be seen and Aviv shook himself, anger replacing his frustration.

'We need to help her now Aviv, before it is too late.' Katya begged.

'I need to make sure Dagon and the King do not survive.'

'If Dagon is dead, so be it, but if he is not, he will be after her.' Katya pointed to the roof and Aviv suddenly began to understand.

'Samson was a distraction to bring Delilah out of hiding. Of course! Why did I not see this coming? She is vulnerable now he is gone.' Sadness touched the merchant as realisation struck. His friend was gone.

The companions left the alley, making their way back down the tunnel and moving quickly to avoid a cave-in.

****

The voice broke the spell and Delilah collected her bow from the ground and drew from her quiver. Not one soldier advanced on her, so picking her target was not difficult.

She scanned behind her as more soldiers encircled her and took a deep breath. The closest man fell with an arrow jutting from his neck. The second was fast but not fast enough. Delilah could tell these men were under orders not to kill her. Dagon wanted her alive.

The thought of that monster sacrificing her daughter and taking her as his queen brought bile to her mouth, but she swallowed hard and continued to rain arrows on her enemy. Her anger at Samson's death was still fresh and fed her rage.

Her quiver was empty and Delilah prayed for Asherah. Where was she? She said she would aid her. She promised to bring help.

Delilah drew her dagger and rose from her archer stance. She turned to check behind for soldiers and then circled like a trapped lion, crouched ready for the next attack.

Her belly was heavy now and her legs quivered with exhaustion. 'I will never give myself to him.' She shouted at the blank faces before her. Each soldier did his duty without question, as if they were in a trance. Delilah would not beg, she could not beg. Dagon was the reason Samson had perished and she would avenge him. She allowed her rage to build, to protect her from the dark angel.

The rush was all at once and within a heartbeat Delilah was unarmed. Hands grabbed at her from all directions, dragging her onto her back by her plaited hair. They pinned her arms to the ground; a man on every limb.

'I will die before he takes me.' She spat on the face of the closest solider who tried to stuff a rag in her mouth. She flung her head to the side and he gripped her jaw, shoving his finger past her gritted teeth until she gagged.

'Enough!' The voice was unmistakeable and the soldiers pulled back, bowing as they moved away. The rooftop was eerily quiet now. The sound of falling rubble had ceased and the temple soldiers did not make a sound, not even a murmur.

Dagon floated toward her like a wisp of wind and Delilah fought his gaze. It was toxic she knew, but intoxicating all the same and no matter how hard she tried, she could not break his hold.

'Samson is gone my dear. Time to let go of your inhibitions.' Dagon waved his hand in the air and drew Delilah up from the stone without touching her. He stared into her eyes and her chin lifted to him like a wanton woman, exposing her neck to tempt the dark angel.

Inside of her mind she raged at Dagon but the scar on her neck tingled with relentless pleasure and her whole body began to tremble with anticipation.

Please Asherah, please! The words did not leave her lips but her mind cried out to be released.

The sound of sword on sword broke the spell and Delilah fell to the ground, crawling on all fours away from Dagon.

'The Nazarite is dead. Let it be peasants. There is no use fighting a god when you are mortal, without power. Even Samson could not defeat me.' Dagon waved his arms as blasts of air surged forward, knocking Katya's men from their feet.

'You are not a god Dagon. We know what you are.' Aviv yelled as he regained his footing.

Katya blocked a thrust to his head as a temple soldier took the opportunity of distraction. Aviv heard the ring above him and turned, sending an upward thrust through the man's groin.

'You know nothing! You are a flea in my hair, a pest to be dealt with.' Dagon circled both his arms above his head and dark clouds began to form. Shards of ice fell from the sky and Katya's men covered their heads to protect themselves.

Sahib shielded Katya with his body as an icicle the size of a dagger flew in her direction. His armour protected him from the full force, but the fragments exploded on impact, sending smaller pieces in all direction, one taking him in the right eye.

He screamed out in pain but quickly replaced the sensation with rage. His uninjured eye seethed with malice and Katya took her bodyguard's arm in warning. 'Not yet!' She whispered and Sahib nodded his understanding.

Chapter 51

'We must go now! Before Dagon takes Delilah.' Asherah tried to keep the panic from her voice, but it was impossible.

'Michael said we must wait. He said you would understand later.' Astarte tried to console her sister.

'Later might work for the Archangel, but I am not a patient warrior. If he does not give the order soon, I will have to go.' Anath's sword sparkled with power and she smiled apprehensively, almost snickering at her own impatience.

The Veil was thin and the sounds of screams could be heard. They had seen the fall of the temple and Asherah had turned away as Samson had disappeared below the weight of a mountain of stone.

Even with the Creator's strength he could not have survived such a heavy weight crushing in on him.

The three angels almost paced as they floated in spirit form. Asherah's hair was suspended like a silk ribbon on the wind and Astarte's fine sheer robes flowed like a rippling stream. Anath wore a short kilt of gold tipped leather and a tightly fitted breast-plate that left nothing to the imagination.

'How do we know when the time is right? Dagon has Delilah *now* and Aviv and Katya are making no headway. If we do not intercede soon, it will be too late. Delilah calls for me. I must answer.' Asherah almost begged her sisters to agree with her, but both stood their ground, sure in Michael's orders.

'He is the Archangel, the leader of our armies but I am done waiting.' Anath patted Asherah on the shoulder. 'Let us go then. Now.' She nodded to Astarte who seemed to give in easily but sighed her agitation none the less.

****

Delilah heard them before she saw them. The sound was like drums in the distance. The goddesses arrived from the sky just as Dagon's daggers of ice had—from nothingness.

Asherah landed next to Delilah and placed herself between the young woman now heavy with child and the dark angel who desired her.

'You have gone too far now brother. The order has been given.'

Dagon frowned as he watched his sisters take their places like a triangle, one in each point. Anath stood with her white and gold sword just to his right, while Astarte floated, unwilling to land, slightly behind his left line of sight.

They were clever, hovering almost outside his vision, while Asherah drew his attention forward, but they were not accustomed to death the way he was.

'You believe three sweet little goddesses are a match for *me*?' Dagon goaded. 'There are no rules of engagement with me Anath and I am not distracted by the haunt of your pure, melodic voice Astarte.'

'What about all of us you black-hearted usurper?' Aviv puffed up his chest and rose from the ground, removing the temple soldier's blood from his sword on the dead man at his feet.

'What do you know of such things mortal? I do not stand here to be judged by humanity.'

'No, you have been judged by Father.' Asherah spoke quietly, with regret she did not realise she felt. 'You forced His hand in this. The Creator has always left you to your meddling but not this time.'

'Why not? What is so important about this little morsel?' Dagon called to Delilah once more and she turned her head away, trying desperately to avoid his gaze. Now that Samson was gone, she could feel Dagon's hold was growing in strength. Soon it would be unbreakable.

'That brother, is none of your business.'

'We will see about that.' The flames left his hand without warning and Asherah's shield was raised too late. The goddess was flung from her feet as Anath rushed forward to shield her from Dagon's attack.

Astarte saw an opening and raised her hand, sending a shower of boiling steam at the dark angel. He was not distracted. He forced the flames closer to Anath with his right hand. Asherah could not rise above her sister's shield. Dagon used his other hand to send the steam back toward Astarte with a blast of air.

The goddess ducked and rolled to her right as the vapour rushed past her. She flew into the air and disappeared into the Veil as Anath took her shield and forced a surge of air back toward Dagon, knocking him from his feet.

'This is not going to be easy sister. Get Delilah out of here.' Anath turned and called to Asherah. She returned her gaze to Dagon too late, the ice blast hit her with full force, sending her over the rooftop and plummeting to the ground below.

'Our turn now. Time to see how you go against mere mortals.' Aviv and Katya began to circle.

'Even better than against goddesses you insignificant ant.' Dagon swung his arms around his head and smiled at his combatants. 'Your friends are not doing so well with my soldiers.' He nodded behind Aviv and Katya.

Katya looked over her shoulder for a heartbeat to see how her men were faring. The temple soldiers were very skilled but many had been injured in the ice attack by Dagon and were now struggling. Katya's archers had taken up positions on adjoining buildings and they peppered the soldiers whenever they got a clean shot.

She realised her mistake too late. The blow took her in the chest and knocked her onto her back. Aviv made to protect his fallen lover but Katya protested. 'Do not dare Aviv. Get that bastard.'

'Feisty. I like feisty. If Delilah does not work out, I might just come back for you.' Dagon chuckled as Aviv snarled.

He knew Dagon was goading him, but it was working. All he had to do was be a distraction long enough to get Katya and Delilah out of this place. He could only hope that Asherah took the opportunity.

'You are wasting my time little man.' Dagon flicked his hand as though he were swatting a fly and Aviv flew into the air, landing heavily enough to be knocked unconscious.

Asherah saw Aviv land, the crack of his head upon the stone was audible. She felt for his energy.

He was alive, but not for long. She saw Sahib moving behind Dagon and warned him with a frown to stay out of sight.

The man was huge and he moved with unnatural stealth for one so large, but he was not invincible and Asherah had seen enough damage already. She needed to get Delilah away from her friends, away from others who might be harmed by Dagon.

'If you want her Dagon, you are going to have to catch her.'

Delilah felt the ground move away from her body and she fought the rising panic. Her stomach did somersaults and her child kicked out at the strange sensation of sudden upward movement.

Dagon watched his queen fly into the air and the confusion was evident in his features. Delilah rose at lightning speed into the Veil and disappeared from his sight.

'You cannot reach her in the Veil brother. You are forbidden to enter.'

'You are forbidden from allowing a human to enter!' Dagon screamed with frustration.

Sahib moved from behind the dark angel who never saw the sword coming from behind. The weapon cleared Dagon's chest, lifting him from his feet.

Dagon touched the blade with his finger and lifted the blood to his lips. Sahib frowned with confusion for only a moment but it was long enough. Dagon drew the sword all the way through his body and swung it like an executioner.

Sahib's head fell to the ground and rolled past Katya who was regaining her footing, and attempting to reach Aviv. The queen of the thieves looked from Aviv's still form on the ground to Sahib's lifeless body and released a blood curdling howl.

'No Katya!' Asherah cried and used every bit of strength she could muster to place a wall of water between her and Dagon.

Dagon rubbed his chest. 'That actually hurt you know?' His manner was casual, conversational. 'How long can you hold that wall in place?'

'Long enough for me to do what is necessary.' Dagon looked above to see Moloch.

'Brother. I was wondering how much longer you might be.' Dagon smiled and waved his hand toward Asherah. 'Do you wish to do the honours?'

'You have gone too far this time brother.' Moloch looked torn and Dagon gazed from him to Asherah who was almost completely focussed on keeping Delilah held in the Veil and Katya trapped behind the wall of water.

'Why did you not bring the girl with you?' Dagon looked confused as Moloch continued to lower himself to the rooftop without aiding him.

Moloch moved towards his brother, a look of agony evident. He looked over his shoulder at Asherah, her face contorted and focussed on saving the humans.

'Because it is over...' The dagger had pierced Dagon's heart and black blood oozed from the wound. Moloch hugged the dark angel to his chest and patted him like a puppy as the life left his eyes.

Asherah gasped as Moloch followed Dagon down to the ground, dropping to his knees—the Flaming Sword in his hands, dripping with Dagon's blood.

'Why?' Dagon coughed as Moloch knelt by his side.

'Meddling with the humans is one thing, but the willingness to kill our sisters is unforgivable, even for me. I never wanted any of this Dagon. This is not the fight I wished for.'

Asherah dropped the wall of water away and Katya rushed to Aviv.

The breath began to rattle in Dagon's throat and the sky opened like a curtain. The light that shone beyond was blinding and Katya covered her eyes for protection.

Delilah floated down, wrapped in the arms of the goddess Astarte. She was no longer conscious but looked unharmed.

Asherah took Delilah and placed her on the ground carefully. 'Please look for Anath. I have felt her essence. She is unconscious below.' Astarte nodded and flew from the building, seeking out her sister.

'Please Asherah, do something.' Katya begged, cradling Aviv's head in her lap and stroking his pale face with her fingertips.

'Of course.' Asherah moved toward Aviv, still not taking her eyes from her dying brother.

Moloch waited until Dagon closed his eyes. He removed the sword—a weapon of legend that had not been seen since the fall. He sheathed it into a place of invisibility.

Asherah dropped down beside Aviv, but could not tear her eyes from Moloch as he cradled his brother in a loving embrace and launched himself into the sky with power and grace. The opening above them seemed to glow brighter as the two angels reached the entrance and even Asherah had to turn her face away.

'How is it he gets into Heaven after what he has done?' Katya was channelling her fear for Aviv into anger at his attacker.

'He is dead Katya. I believe Moloch returns him to the Father so they can all mourn his loss.'

'He is a demon. After what he has done to Aviv, he does not deserve to be mourned by anyone.' Katya's nostrils flared with her frustration.

'Even your worst enemy will be mourned by those who loved him.' The goddess returned her gaze to Aviv. She touched his forehead and closed her eyes, summoning her energy to the heroic merchant. A smile spread across her face as she felt his heartbeat grow stronger.

Epilogue

'Must you take her now? So soon!' Delilah wiped the sweat from her brow as the sound of a new-born cry filled the darkened room.

'The only way this can possibly succeed if she is delivered now, as a new-born.' Asherah's eyes were soft.

Delilah gently lifted her daughter to her bare chest and wiped the wetness away from her matted curls. Tears streamed down her face as she returned her gaze to the goddess.

'Can I feed her?'

'No Delilah. I am so sorry. There is not enough time.'

'Where are you taking her?' Delilah's eyes grew fearful as she wrapped the baby girl in a shawl of muslin and kissed her tiny button nose.

'Best you do not know. She will be loved. She will be safe from Moloch and those that might want to harm her. She is part of a prophecy that will bring peace to earth and the eternal realm.'

'I hope that you are right Asherah, for this sacrifice is great.'

'You have no idea how many more such precious sacrifices will be made in aid of this cause.' Asherah sat down next to Delilah and reached out to touch her arm gently. 'What will you call her?'

'I can give her a name?' Delilah's eyes sparkled with a joy she had not felt since long before Samson had died. Choosing to give up her daughter had been the hardest decision she had ever made, harder than watching Samson die—harder than leaving her family behind. She understood the danger to them both if she did not, but after all she had been through, it was heart-breaking.

'Of course you can. She is your child and the woman who will care for her has just given birth herself. She will respect your wishes. Your daughter is to become one of two royal twins and only the mother and the nurse will know the truth of her birth.'

Delilah cradled the baby girl and closed her eyes as she took a deep, contemplative breath. She imagined Samson in her mind. His face was strong and courageous and she willed herself to be as he was. 'I will call her Ruth.'

Asherah smiled softly and reached for the baby girl. 'Ruth it shall be then.'

Dedication

My writing is heavily steeped in a deep desire to explore theology in every culture. For now, I prefer an historical setting because I believe we have so much to learn from our past victories and even more so, from our mistakes.

I dedicate this book to my husband George, whose good-natured cynicism rubbed off on this naïve young woman who thought she could change the world. What he has helped me to understand is that everyone sees the world from their own perspective. So now, when I write, I put myself in the spirit of each character and see how they would see themselves. Without this gift, my writing would never have come to be.

What Next!

If this is the first book of mine you have picked up, then why not go back and start at the beginning. My first series – *Covenant of Grace* – is complete and you can start your journey with book 1– *Destiny of Kings* free. Just tell me where to send it by signing up on my website at www.atime2write.com.au

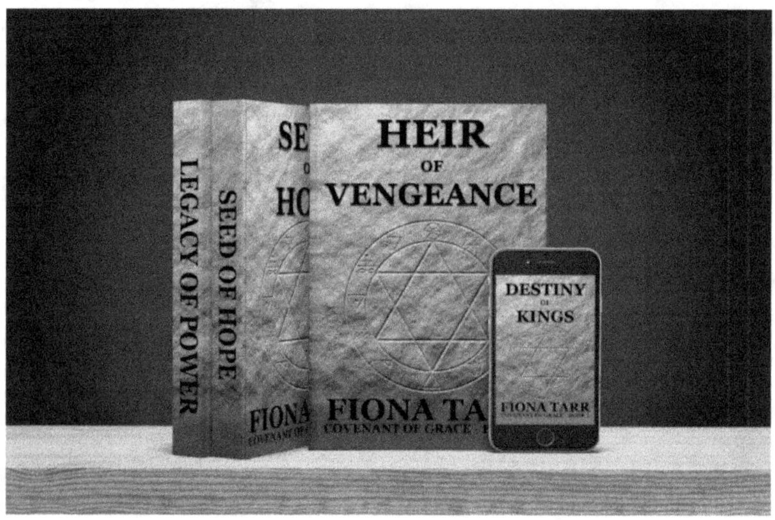

To find out more about my current work, you can follow me on Facebook or find me on my website atime2write.com.au

Thanks again for reading.

Reviews!

As an Indie Author I don't have an expensive story editor (just a very good copy editor) or a team of professionals to help me with my work, so reviews are important to me. They help me develop my writing style and they help others decide if buying one of my books is worth their effort, but most of all, reviews are what keep me typing into the night and publishing my work.

To leave a review, just return to your online book seller and tell me what you thought of Delilah and the Dark God.

Books by Fiona Tarr

The Eternal Realm Series

Book 1 – The Jericho Prophecy

Book 2 – Delilah and the Dark God

****

The Priestess Chronicles Series

Book 1 – Call of the Druids

****

The Covenant of Grace Series

Book 1 – Destiny of Kings

Book 2 – Seed of Hope

Book 3 – Legacy of Power

Book 4 – Heir of Vengeance

Prequel – The Ehud Dagger

Boxed set of all 5 – The Complete Collection